Freedom of the Souls

Ancient Gods

Sinai Cardenas

Copyright © Sinai Cardenas, 2021

This paperback edition first published in 2021

Cover design on fiverr.com rock_0407

ISBN 978-1-955967-00-6

Sinai Cardenas

5949 Camp Road#1159 Hamburg, NY 14075

HTTP://mssinaicardenas.wixsite.com/blog

Acknowledgments

A seven-year-old girl wrote a crappy letter, and in the last sentence, she stated that she was going to write a book one day. It was always a distant dream. She kept writing for herself, filling notebooks with unfinished stories and word documents that got lost. Some did reach a virtual platform named Wattpad, but that is as far as she went. Now, I can tell that little girl that we made it, thanks to my family's support, and that this is just the beginning.

It was always in the back of my mind, as a long-term dream. However, it seems that the universe had other plans for me. Everything came into place to focus on writing, and I did even when I had no more imagination to extract. I'm grateful to all the people that support me and encourage me throughout this journey. Especially to my brothers Cesar, Moises, and Tobias, this story wouldn't have existed without them.

When I started this process, I learned a few lessons. The first one is that I would always pay the price for my ignorance when starting something new. Thankfully, I was able to get a refund on this occasion. The second one is that nothing is perfect, so trying to fix every little detail would take me nowhere; it's better to enjoy the journey and accept the mistakes. The last lesson and most valuable of all is that when you figure out what you truly want and are not afraid of saying it out loud, the universe conspires in your favor.

There were a lot of setbacks and fear. Most of the time, I thought I wasn't going to make it. But thanks to my parents, my sisters Dalma and Belen, who encouraged me, I was able to continue. And also, thanks to my other two sisters Isabel and Teresa, for their constant support.

Emotions, many of them are needed to write. They are the fuel of any story. So, having this in mind, I would also like to thank N.N., who gave me such a heartbreak that motivated me to pour all my sadness and anger into the pages of this book.

Prologue

It was an early day in the fields; the morning gave a sense of peace and calm. The birds sounded happier than usual, and the sun's rays started caressing the crops, warming the earth. It seemed that this would be a perfect day. However, in a split second, everything changed. The sky obscured, and a sudden ball of light made the sun resemble a piece of ornament whose function was obsolete. The man —the only man who was doing his job harvesting crops— lost his eyesight momentarily by the brightness of the light. Then as soon as it happened, it disappeared, leaving no trace behind. The sky came back to its standard color, and just as the man began to think it had all been a hallucination from thirst, a tremendous sound erupted. The land beneath the man's feet shook. After that, everything went quiet; even the wind stood still.

A mist began to form in broad daylight. The man stood mesmerized by such an occurrence. The fog danced and separated as if it were a living thing making a path for a tall and slim silhouette to pass. The way it moved, it appeared to have a purpose in mind, a place to go, and it did not attempt to approach the man. It just walked by. The man stood there petrified, watching the events, trying to understand. Then the mist dissolved, and everything went back to how it began. That simple fact terrified the man to the point of running towards the Olmec altepetl.

As he reached the lord, he collected himself, but his voice betrayed him "Tecuhtli, Tecuhtli, I, I-"

"Speak up, boy. We don't have time to waste. The huentli is upon us, and we shall make it perfect" Tecuhtli had such a grave gaze that it made the man tense and speechless "Come on, boy, speak!"

"In the fields, something fell from the sky, and then a shadow floated," said the boy, articulating each word slowly, almost as if he was trying to convince himself of what he saw.
Tecuhtli immediately took the man by the elbow and dragged him outside where no one could hear "Repeat that"

"I saw something crashing into the outer fields and a shadow passing. It was heading somewhere."

"Are you certain of this?" Tecuhtli's voice was flat with a hint of concern

"Yes, the land trembled as it hit the earth and, and there was mist and-"

"Enough!" Tecuhtli paced back and forth, his mind collecting all sorts of thoughts. What if it was a sign that the gods were angry? Or maybe they sent a terrible misfortune as the old scrolls described.

"Listen to me, go to where the light hit, and take a mental note of everything you see. Do this discreetly, then come straight back to me."

The man did as he was instructed —much against his will. Taking his tools, he headed back to the fields with shaking hands and his mind replaying the earlier events thinking, what if the shadow came back and attacked him? How would he defeat it? He had never been brave, nor had the complexion of a warrior. He had a much simpler job; being a farmer provided him a safe life. No risks, no trouble.

Reaching the impact zone and expecting to find a crater or at least some type of damage, he finds the land intact. However, to his astonishment, a serpent with encrusted feathers around its head lay in the middle of the field. Indeed, this was no ordinary serpent; he had never seen a reptile similar to this. Even at a safe distance, he could see how it changed in different colors, which could only mean it was more significant than usual. It didn't seem alive; it didn't move, which indicated that it was safe for the man to approach. Curiosity invaded him as he was getting closer and, involuntarily, he slowly stretched his hand, aching for the touch of that serpent. And just as he did, a dark liquid, like black ink, began covering his hands, inducing excruciating pain as it advanced. It was clear that he was screaming, but there was no sound coming out, just a hint of agony showing in his face as the ink spread to each part of his body, much like his blood coursing through his veins. Finally, he collapsed, convulsing in the ground, saliva coming out of his mouth, his eyes turning white, and his mind, his mind just went blank.

As his body lay there, under the cold night sky, helpless against the attack of any beast, two figures approached the man.

There was no ink and no serpent, no evidence of what had happened or why a farmer man was on the ground unconscious. They decided to take him back to the Olmec altepetl, from where they assumed he belonged.

Tecuhtli recognized the body that the men carried and immediately instructed them to put him in the petatl on the floor inside Tecuhtli's chantli. As soon as the men left, Tecuhtli tried to awaken the man "Naran, Naran!" It was the first time he used the name of whom he called 'boy' before, maybe he expected a reaction of some sort, but there was no movement, no indication that Naran could hear him. Yet his heart was beating, and that was enough for now. Eventually, Tecuhtli gave up waiting, leaving the chantli for the night.

Morning came slowly and almost seemed to be doing it on purpose. Naran lay still, his chest rising and falling in coordination with his breathing. A ray of sun sneaks in, trying to find the perfect place to let its light shine. It then stumbles in Naran's feet, waking him. He felt fine and unaware that his eyes had changed. They were pitch black, like an obsidian marble that reflects no light. Then, after a few seconds, they went back to normal. He sat up, feeling his bones crack, complaining of the abrupt disruption after a long nap. While outside, Tecuhtli spoke with a stranger whose voice made the heart of Naran tingle.

"He has been sleeping."

"I'm just going to make sure he is fine," As the stranger entered the chantli, every particle on Naran's body shivered. "Hello, Naran," the way the stranger moved with his shadow lagging behind him made Naran realize that he had seen the stranger before. The only difference was that this time there was no mist. Immediately he attempted to get up, scream, and run away, but it was just that, an attempt. The stranger laughed at Naran's useless efforts. "Ignorant human, there is no point in fighting it," the stranger's voice was firm and shallow. He moved around the chantli with an air of superiority, his hands folded on his back, and his face —especially his eyes— were so intimidating that Naran couldn't bear his gaze for long.

"Who, who are you?"

He paced, looking at his hands. It seemed he was admiring them. Then he directed his gaze at the only ray of sun that was in the chantli. "It's interesting how simple the human mind is." The beam of light moved quickly towards the stranger, following an unheard command. He began to manipulate it so that Naran had to rub his eyes to make sure he saw clearly. The ray of light moved back and forth, and then it turned into a solid sphere of light floating in circles around the chantli. "I am the eternal sun. A god, if you will," the globe approached the god's face, giving a glimpse to Naran of the true self of the supposed god. His pale, radiant face, every bone so defined and sharp; his eyes full of an intense light that resembled the sun's brightness, and his hair that seemed to be floating around his head. "You insignificant human will serve me, and if you do it well, I may let you live." The sphere went directly at Naran's head; he tried desperately to block it with his hands. However, the globe went right through, and just like that, his body stopped responding.

The god bent down and touched Naran's chest right above the heart. "This might hurt," the god chuckled. "It's going to be the worst pain you will ever experience." Instantly Naran screamed in agony. The pain was way worse than when the ink consumed his body, and surprisingly, no one heard, not even Tecuhtli, who was right outside. "Get up." Naran obeyed, ignoring entirely what he just experienced, and stood firm in front of the god. "We are going to cleanse this world from darkness." The god put his hand on Naran's shoulder and smiled, giving him a sense of peace.

They stepped out of the chantli, where Tecuhtli approached them with an intense gaze. "Naran, you are awake! What happened?" He said, eager to know what Naran saw the previous day and why he was unconscious in the fields. It was impossible for them to simply ignore Tecuhtli and continue walking, which exasperated the god, who turned to look directly at his eyes. "Silent," he ordered, then he touched the side of Tecuhtli's head with a similar version of the sphere he used in Naran, but this one was flat and smaller with a sharp end. "Naran never existed," he whispers, and just like that, as simple as that, the god erases every memory of Naran in Tecuhtli's mind.

Chapter 1

The Olmec altepetl was the most ancient of all; therefore, respect was of the most importance. Their land had the most prominent crop fields, and even though there was a strong hierarchy among the people, there was an enormous amount of peace. The probable reason behind the harmony in the altepetl is that the elders molded the children's brains to suit specific tasks. Meaning that from birth, everyone knew what to do and what was expected of them. Naran was no exception. He was content harvesting crops; he enjoyed working with his hands and providing for the altepetl. The thought of fighting or going to battles terrified him. However, there was a time when 'adventurous' and reckless were the perfect words to describe him. He could go into the river and dive, not caring if the riff was too strong; he knew somehow, he could make it out safely. As the years passed, fear began filling his heart. He began to focus on the fragility of existence, developing an irrational fear of dying. Therefore, every time the elders asked him to do something new or command him a different task than his usual activities, he was conflicted. A million thoughts about how everything could go wrong clouded his head, making it difficult for him to communicate and behave freely with others.

The preparation the Tecuhtli was upholding in the Olmec altepetl was a type of huentli for the fire god. Every year the altepetl turned upside down, making sure that the celebration honoring the god, as a thank you for not releasing upon them the perpetual night —at least that's what generation after generation has been taught—, was perfect to the last detail. This meant that there was a lot to do, and all hands had to be occupied, meaning that Naran had to be alone in the fields. It was not the first time and surely will not be the last, however for some reason, he couldn't bring himself to do it, to get out of the chantli early in the morning and do the job he has done for years.

"It's another day," he said to himself with a small voice that barely reached his ears. Then, putting his breechcloth and tying around his neck —what used to be— a white sheet, "you should be thankful not to be a slave." He said under his breath. Then, picking up a basket that was made by braiding plants, he headed towards the field. Next, he started to chant his usual mantra when he was scared or fatigued by the routine. *You should be thankful not to be a slave.*

A few kilometers away from any civilization in a distant crop field, a serpent stood in the middle of a strange land yet somewhat familiar to it. Without moving, it adjusts its vision, trying to absorb the environment. When the smell of the trees and petrichor hit its nostrils, it triggers memories that turn into flashbacks making it realize where it was. "I never thought I would be here again," the resonant voice suggests a young human male trapped in the skin of a serpent.

Struggling to a resting position made his extremities uncomfortable. It wasn't often he could get out of his prison and move freely. "Did that bastard finally achieve sufficient energy? Is that why he came here?" The question hid a hint of concern. Could it be that deep down, he wanted him to fail? He dismisses the thought quickly, recalling he has no choice but to comply. He moved around as if he was searching for something and was disappointed to find only dirt and trees. Feeling frustrated by his animal form, he slid upwards, reaching the top of a tree. "After all I did for him, he still chooses to treat me like a pet." It took a moment to scan the land just to find it deserted, "Have humans gone extinct?" The answer to his question appeared in the distance; a human figure started to get closer. He could perceive it was a male human —and as difficult as it was to do so — a slim curve line on its lips appeared, indicating a sudden joy of having found the perfect vase without even looking for it. Knowing how manipulable humans can be, he slid down and began transforming its exterior to appear as he did many centuries ago. Its skin went from a light green into a darker one with traces of black; around its head, multiple large feathers from different colors started to appear, and when the wind brushes against them, it creates the illusion they have changed to rose gold color.

When the human took a step inside the sensorial circle of the serpent, an electrical wave crossed its body, making him feel uneasy and on edge. *Could it be that he is more than just a vase?* The thought made him almost stop luring the human. *Maybe this is a setup.* Unfortunately, it was too late to change plans. The male human, unable to resist, reached his hand towards the head of the serpent. The human absorbed the reptile body, and as it began to fade, so did his worries. The only remaining thought, as it vanished, was that finally, he would be able to live again.

Chapter 2

Naran kept walking behind the god at a respectful distance, feeling different, more alive than ever. He could feel the air and even the particles of light hitting his skin. They had been walking for hours under the sun, and he felt no agitation, had no sweat, and more importantly, no thirst. Strangest of all was that every time his bare feet made contact with the grass, a sensation like no other navigated from the tip of his toes to his ears. It felt like a sort of euphoria dripping straight from his heart. *Shouldn't this be a good feeling?* He wondered as he remembered the morning before he couldn't bring himself out of the chantli. If all these new sensations were good, why did he feel uneasy? Touching his forehead for the tenth time to see if there were drops of sweat — yet again, there was nothing.

Unable to bear the question any longer, the words spurt out of his mouth. "Did you do something to me?" Nara spoke so quickly and clearly that he stood still, amazed that he said that without a hint of hesitation.

"I have evaporated your fears. You should thank me," said the god with a calm and relaxed voice. It never occurred to Naran that fears could be erased. Every time he tries acting bravely before he does something risky, a feeling of fear crosses his entire body. However, here he was, feeling serene and at ease in front of a smiling god. "Thank you," Naran said under his breath, catching up with the god.

Unaware of where they were heading, Naran kept moving his legs and arms, crouching and then making small jumps, as if experiencing being in his body for the first time. Then, abruptly, the god stopped, making Naran collapse against him. He quickly took a step back as the god turned to see him and pointed, "Teotihuacan is up ahead somewhere in the distance."

"What are we doing here?" said Naran as he recognized the road and the entrance of the altepetl.

"I told you there is darkness in this world, and cleansing it is up to us. Well, to me. However, I have decided to make you part of this grand job."

Suppose someone had told Naran earlier this morning that he would battle against an unknown threat, with no preparation, no fighting skills, and not an ounce of courage. A job that never crossed his mind, which meant a new thing to do, his heart would have started to beat faster, his palms would become sweaty, anxiety would have shown in his face, and an overpowering fear would freeze him in the spot. Yet, none of that happened this time. Instead, he felt full of energy and eager to get started. "How are we going to do that?" he asked.

The god approached Naran, putting his arm around him, and said with a bright smile, "not 'we' This will be your quest." Naran kept quiet, unsure how to respond or if he heard correctly.

What could he do against the darkness when he was a mere

human? "You met my lovely pet in the morning. It is a bit playful but has great power. And now, it's inside you." Even though this was an answer to Naran's earlier question, it only confused him because of how the god said those words, as if this was something that happened every day. "The serpent you saw on the fields, I knew that you would find it, and I was expecting that my pet would find you... appealing enough to make you it's home." The memory of the dark inky liquid spreading through his body made Naran shiver. What exactly did this mean? Even if he had the snake inside of him, he was no fighter. The god continued talking, not caring for the confusion showing in Naran's face. "Teotihuacan reeks of evil, and this is where you shall begin. Upon entering, you will encounter thousands of demons, disturbing creatures that resemble reptiles. Thankfully humans cannot see them, except for you. Now go and just let your instincts act, and you will be fine." The confidence that the god had in Naran was strange; they had just met. There was also the fact that he was a god, which made it nonsensical to send a farmer to do his job. Not to mention that Naran felt no instincts whatsoever, and even if he were to handle them, what could instincts do against such hideous monsters?

"There is one thing missing," the god said, looking at Naran from head to toe. He grabbed what seemed like a ray of light and one leaf that fell to the ground. He then shaped it into a thin and longer tecpatl.

The deep black color of the blade and its thinness were entirely on a different level than those made of wood and jade that Naran knew. "What a strange-looking tecpatl!"

"It's called a sword," said the god as he handed the sword to Naran, and to his surprise, it was heavier than he anticipated. But, thinking that it was all he needed, Naran turned and started walking towards the altepetl.

"Not done yet," the god stops him, "You also need to look like a savior."

With a quick flicker of the god's hand, Naran's garments started to transform. His body became fully clothed with a combination of the Teopixqui and the Tecuhtli traditional attire. He felt a cape hanging from his neck and laying on his right shoulder. Instead of the breechcloth that narrowly covered his body, there was a long white cloth that covered his shoulders to his hips. Red fabric in his waist stretched below his thighs. Around his neck, there was a golden ornament that almost covered his shoulders and two bracelets in his upper arms. The best part —to Naran, that is— was that he was no longer barefoot. Unable to resist his curiosity Naran ran to a nearby pond to see his reflection. When he saw himself, he noticed that his features resembled a warrior with solid hands, broad shoulders, light brown skin, and a prominent jawline; even his eyes that used to be brown were now beautiful emerald green. A bright smile appeared on his face. He turned to see the god, standing straight, feeling taller than usual.

"This will provide a disguise. It's easier than me going around and making people forget your face." The god took one last look at his pupil and left, not giving any further instructions.

Standing in the middle of the road, about thirty steps away from the Teotihuacan altepetl, Naran took a deep breath, and slowly with small steps, he began to walk. With his gesture, he reveals his obvious affliction, the result of his mind going in circles and his heart telling him that something was wrong. Nevertheless, a god had come to him and chose him to do this quest. And as far as he knows, gods do not harm you unless you betray them. After all, that is what every adult had told him since he was a kid. So, how could that not be true?

When he was a few steps away from the entrance of the altepetl, the first thing he noticed was that there were no people around. The altepetl seemed deserted. He took another step forward and a small creature, the size of a dog, crawled slowly towards his feet. It did not resemble a reptile, at least not one that Naran has ever seen. The skin on half of its body was missing, and it had a hole where the right eye should have been. With his single eye staring at Naran, the creature blinked, making Naran feel disgusted. He took the sword and slashed the demon's head with a clean cut. The headless body shook for a moment until it gave out.

Staring at the lifeless creature, thinking of how quickly he had responded, without hesitation; how right the sword felt in his hand, and how gracefully he used it, made him believe that this is who he was meant to be all along. Could it be that having his fears erased had unchained his potential? *Set fire to the body,* a voice similar to the god's, instructed. He looked behind him, expecting to find the god, but there was no one. Naran wondered about the possibility that the god had gone invisible and was right next to him. However, the most plausible answer was that they had a mental connection that let him hear the god, which means that the god can see everything Naran does. "It would make sense. He is the Sun, after all." He answered his question out loud, making his heart skip a beat when he heard his deep and firm voice. Composing himself, he took the limbs and dragged them into the woods. Trying to find the perfect place where no one would notice the smoke and he could do as instructed, now all he needed was to start the fire.

Gathering different sizes of wood, putting them on top of the body, placing a few dry leaves at the bottom, and with two texcalli, he created enough friction to produce sparkles. *It would be easier if you let me do this for you.* The god's voice startled Naran, making him drop the texcalli. It was strange to hear him in his head, "where are you?"

Here. A long shadow dripped from Naran's hands as if it was pure darkness made of liquid. It slid on the floor and transformed into a serpent. "We meet again," it said with a voice that resembled the god. However, this one was shallower and raspier. It stood in a defying pose with its head at the same level as Naran's eyes, "I can create fire for you." Standing there looking straight into Naran's face, without making any movement towards the pile woods, the fire started, startling Naran, who fell on his back. "How did you do that?!" Even though he had been shocked, he did not feel scared.

"Humans call it magic. I call it ability," The serpent slithered around its limbless body began contorting and changing form into what appeared to be a human shape, save for a few differences. Everything on its face was missing except for the eyes, and its body reflected no light. It was as if a shadow had become solid,

"I don't like to be out of my home," It walked and sat next to Naran, who was still on the floor, not sure of what he saw, "I can't do my part if you reject me." The thought that this thing had been inside of him all this time made him sick to his stomach, and he gagged. The fact that nothing had come out reminded him that his stomach was empty because he had not eaten in two days. "Ugh! Humans are so disgusting!"

Naran composed himself, wiping his mouth with the back of his hand, and sat up straight, "why do you sound like the Sun?"

"He is me, and I'm him."

"What does that mean?"

The shadowy figure rested its chin on its hand "humans are also stupid!" he said. It amazes Naran that the shadow had no mouth, yet they are having a conversation. *How is this possible? Why does the voice of that thing sound so clear inside my head?* Naran wonders. "I'm not human, nor animal. I'm not from your physical world," keeping his eyes locked on Naran, "you still don't understand?" feeling vulnerable, Naran moved his head, not wanting to speak, "I prefer a verbal human" Naran swallowed.

He reminded himself that he was different now. With that in mind, he tried to get the courage he felt before, yet the laughter from the shadowy figure overtook his attempt. "It was me who made you brave" It stood up and walked towards the fire. "You are nothing without me." Naran expected it to see the flames through it or see any color. However, there was only blackness. The thing kept walking until it was standing in the middle of the fire. "The only good thing about a human is their sensations" It stayed there looking at Naran, inviting him into the flames, mocking him for his lack of courage. Could it be that his fears were back? He stood up and froze, unable to make any more movements. "I have my mind; my actions. I do not follow the orders of the 'god,' as you call him."

Naran found his voice somewhere inside of him. "I didn't have to burn that creature, right?" it was still deep and firm, so that meant that he was indeed different.

"You had to; unless you want it to go back to its normal form."

"I cut that creature's head off. How could it go back?"

The thing walked out of the flames and lifted its index finger, extinguishing the fire, the creature started to shake, and filaments of what looked like blood began running from the head to the body. The way the filaments twisted and slid to make it whole again was the most disturbing thing —aside from the shadowy figure before him— Naran had ever seen. The thing lifted the same finger, and the flames erupted again, and the creature's body stopped drawing blood, becoming a corpse once more.

"Now, do you believe me?" The thing sat in front of the fire, its head tilted up, and its hands were in the ground supporting its upper body. "I don't like this place."

"Then, why are you here?"

The thing turned to look at Naran, its eyes were a bit white, and they also did not reflect any light. "There are things that we must do that we don't like."

"Do you have a name?"

The thing's eyes widened, then looked at the sky. It's hard for Naran to read facial expressions of something that does not have a face. "I'm the Sun."

"You mean the god that I met earlier? But you are different from him."

"Ok, I'm the shadow of the Sun."

"Then Shadow is your name?"

"No stupid human! I don't have a name."

"The Sun calls you, its pet. Doesn't that make you inferior?" That last word made the flames of the fire enlarge, the thing got up, and in the blink of an eye, it stood before Naran. "I am not inferior!"

Every particle on Naran's body shook, and for the first time since the god made him who he is, he felt fear. The type of fear that freezes you on the spot and that darkens your thoughts. "I-I...my apologies."

The thing relaxed and start to walk around. It seems to be thinking —or maybe planning a way to kill Naran. "I would let this pass if you let me have your body." Naran's legs gave out, and he stumbled into a sitting position. Thinking that this was a trick, this shadow thing was also a demon; his first instinct was to run. He then recalled that the god had told him that the serpent was on their side. Though this serpent seemed like it could do whatever it wanted, at least that's what it claimed. So, if Naran agreed and gave his body as requested, what would happen to Naran? And, what about the instructions the god left? How could he achieve them if his body belonged to someone else? "I can tell you are struggling with this." The thing sat down right in front of Naran, making him feel uncomfortable and frightened. "I can become your instincts. I can provide you with abilities. And in return, you will let me eat, drink, and feel everything this useless world provides."

"How could this be possible?"

The thing put its index finger on Naran's forehead. "If you could understand more than what humans have taught you. See the world from a pair of fresh eyes not contaminated by any human belief. Then maybe you would be able to become a god."

Naran's mind started to collect all the information, weighing every possible outcome and what could go wrong. "I will tell you, my name." Suddenly Naran's mind stopped wondering, and he focused all his attention on the thing. "Quetzalcoatl." The familiarity that the name gave Naran made him give up all worries and feel at ease. Without knowing why, he stretched out his hand, Quetzalcoatl took it rapidly. *What's the worst that could go wrong?* Naran thought.

Chapter 3

Waking up to an extreme feeling of thirst, unsure of when he fell asleep, Naran ran towards the sound of a creek. He finally reaches the river, feeling like he was not getting there fast enough to end his misery. Immediately submerges, not caring if it had been a long time since he swam —or had been near a river for that matter—, meaning he had a high possibility of drowning. It took him a few minutes to feel full.

Realizing he could hold his breath for a long time underwater, Naran began to wonder if this could be one of the abilities Quetzalcoatl mentioned; and if so, was he becoming a human fish? He pondered while swimming around, diving, and floating, which was hard to do on sweet water. After a few hours, he stepped out of the water, noticing his wet clothes. "They will dry eventually," he said to himself, dismissing his worries and began to look for his sword. It was then he remembered that he had left it near the bonfire. He headed back, wondering if the thirst he had felt earlier and been able to hold his breath underwater was caused by Quetzalcoatl. If so then, it meant that he could continue to live his life normally.

For some reason, he had thought that once Quetzalcoatl

possessed his body, his consciousness was going to be in some sort of dark place, a trap, where he would be unable to move and just be a witness forever. However, he felt normal. Nothing seemed out of the ordinary, except that the night seemed brighter than usual; that he could hear every sound that the forest provided; and had this urge to be barefoot again —but then again nothing else too out of the ordinary—. Suddenly, concerned that he may be dreaming and trapped, he grabbed the sword and started to make a few swings. Unaware that he was getting closer to a tree with each swing of the blade, with hardly any force, he made a clean cut through the tree trunk —so he was a little different after all.

Though admiring the smell of the tree leaves for the tenth time was slowing Naran, he couldn't help it. He felt a compulsion to stop and smell each one, even though they were precisely the same as the previous ones. These actions reminded Naran of a child who is seeing the world for the first time. Although trees are not relevant, right now, he has a quest to finish! It doesn't matter that the Sun never gave him a time frame; he wanted to be done with it in the shortest time possible.

Losing his patience and feeling irritated with himself, Naran decided to find a way to communicate with Quetzalcoatl and confront him about this childish attitude he was experiencing. "Quetzalcoatl?" he said, hesitant about the type of response he would get back. "Quetzalcoatl!" He said again, although this time louder.

Ugh! What do you want? The now-familiar voice filled Naran's head.

"You're slowing us down. The god gave us orders that we need to obey."

Oh, I'm sorry! Wait, not true. That's your problem, not mine, and he does not order me around! The simultaneously mocking and defensive tone made Naran feel a bit anxious. "But you said-"

I only agreed to share my abilities. You now have strength, and other things, so I kept my end of the bargain!
Naran remained quiet. He couldn't understand how it was that though these two entities were the same, Quetzalcoatl felt aggressive and indifferent, yet the Sun, just with a glance, made him feel joy and calmness. "The god said that you would help me."

'The god said you would help me' Listen, human! *I don't care about what that bastard says. We made a deal, and I did my part, now leave me alone!* The way he mimicked what Naran said made it clear that Quetzalcoatl was taking a very childish attitude. Nonetheless, they had made a deal, and in a way, he was simply sharing his body.

Naran kept walking towards the altepetl, fighting with all his willpower the urge to climb a tree, sit on one of the branches, and watch the night slowly changing colors becoming a sunrise.

"You can see the sunrise later; duty comes first." He told himself. He could almost see the upset look Quetzalcoatl must be having, and the thought of that shadowy figure having a tantrum was a bit disturbing and gratifying at the same time.

Naran tightened his grip on his sword, repeating over and over, 'Duty comes first. Duty comes first.' He never dared to break a rule or go against what he was instructed to do. He had to follow orders; otherwise, he would be punished. Recalling the 15-year-old Naran that had broken the rules and the consequences reinforced the thought of following orders now more than ever. Back then, his mother had sacrificed herself to earn forgiveness for Naran's actions, and since that moment, he became tame and unable to disobey authority.

The memory of the tears in his mother's eyes made him stop.

So, is this why you became a coward?

"That's none of your business!"

Ooh, look who became feisty. Did I hit a nerve?

"Enough!" Naran's strong voice made the birds near a tree flee, fearing for their lives. Clearing his mind and focusing on the present, he accepted his situation, he had been given a job by a god, and he could not refuse it or ignore it.

As he roamed around, he realized Teotihuacan was not a tiny altepetl like the Toltec, which meant that Naran could not do the quest in a matter of two or three days. Out of all the six altepetl, this one was the biggest and most populated, which would make it hard to fight without raising any suspicions. Even if he could see demons, he would need to fight; and to other people, Naran may appear to be a crazy man swinging his shiny sword against an invisible threat. Walking behind the chantli and inhaling deeply, he hesitated for a second, considering abandoning the quest. He heard Quetzalcoatl's voice that, with exasperation, told him *Oh please, would you relax!* This made him feel thankful that this time, he was not alone.

A strong scent invades his nose as he walks closer to the chantli. It was the most disgusting odor he had ever encountered. It reminded him of a dead animal that has been rotting under the sun for an extended period. Following the smell, he discovered a human-sized demon with skin and teeth missing, lurking inside one of the chantli. This one was slightly different from the first one; it had a few hairs on the head, thick blood dripping from its body, and it dropped pieces of rotten skin and flesh as it walked. It stood still, looking directly at Naran's eyes.

Kill it already!

The creature opened its hideous mouth, and a sudden rush took over Naran's body. With the sword in his hand, he pierced the creature's chest right where a heart should have been —if that thing had one—

Remember to-

"Yes, I know. Burn the body!" said Naran, interrupting Quetzalcoatl. Closing his eyes, Naran began to feel a warm sensation traveling down his fingers. A roaring fire came out from his hands when he opened them and streamed down towards the creature's lifeless body. Amazed by what he was doing, suddenly panic began to hit his head, and he took a step back, worried he would catch on fire himself.

Relax! You won't get hurt. Quetzalcoatl's assuredness calmed Naran's heart. This whole experience was so extraordinary that Naran's brain couldn't grasp the idea that this was real. The flames began to increase even more, bringing Naran to the present, and he watched with horror the chantli burning, knowing full well that this would alarm the people around.

Imagine an apaztli made of fire covering the body. Naran closed his eyes and did as told, maintaining the fire, protecting only the length of the demon's body. As he was heading out, another creature rushed into the chantli, Naran reacted instantly, cutting it and burning the pieces, and he stepped out before the chantli fully caught fire.

For a moment, Naran wonders if he should go to each chantli and look for demons. Afraid he would cause a commotion, he stood motionless outside one of the chantli. All sorts of thoughts cross his mind, including retreating and hoping the god would not punish him. Then, as an answer to his concern, a boy appeared. Naran instructed the young man to spread the danger from the demons and evacuate the altepetl towards the fields. He waited inside an empty chantli for some time; then, he continued his job.

After the fifth chantli, Naran became used to finding all kinds of creatures. Some were children's size, some were full-grown men, and others seemed to just decompose in front of his eyes before becoming a recognizable shape. Thanks to Quetzalcoatl, he did not feel tired or agitated, which encouraged him to think it was possible to clean the whole altepetl in less than a week.

He continued with his task, approaching the creatures and killing them before they could react.

Don't you think it's weird? The familiar voice said, making his sword stop, mid-air, right when he was about to strike.

"What's weird?"

They don't attack you.

"That's because I'm quicker." Although what Quetzalcoatl said made him pause, he reasoned that nothing could be wrong if he made such quick work of these creatures.

It was a relief that normal humans could not see them. He kept working diligently, all day, without stopping for water, sleep, or food. When night fell, almost half of the altepetl was free of demons. Unfortunately, some chantli burned down. He had much to learn about his new abilities. They were so unique that he was not able to control them properly. He tried asking Quetzalcoatl for help; however, there was no response as if he had gone to sleep.

The devastation, and desolation, that the sun reveals as it rises on the horizon is the price one pays to win a war; at least, that is what Naran thought as he stared at the altepetl. Every chantli was either a pile of ashes or hardly standing, full of black soot, making him grieve his actions. Naran's last consolation was that people were safe.

Although the war was not over yet. Naran never cared for anyone's wellbeing, yet seeing all the creatures surrounding the Tecuhtli's chantli, made Naran feel a sense of responsibility and a boost of determination to end this battle since he was the only one who could do something about it. "I will save Tecuhtli from all of you!" His strong voice made the words echo in the empty land. There was no trace of fear on Naran's face; however, the demons that held knives and wooden sticks stood their ground and began surrounding him.

Are you sure you want to do this? Quetzalcoatl's voice decided to grace Naran with its presence. "I will not hesitate. Can't you see how disgusting they are?" he said as he tightened the grip of his sword dripping with blood. The demons took a few swings towards Naran, but it was pointless; he was faster than them. His movements were sharp and calculated. The way he handled the sword made it seem as if he had been training all his life.

Heads began to roll in the ground. Hands flying in all directions. Legs collapsing with big wet thuds and blood splashing everywhere. When he finished, Naran was out of breath for the first time since he had met the god.

Quetzalcoatl's perspective

Chapter 4

The night surrounded the forest. The sound of the wind
going through the trees under a clear sky, and a full moon,
created the perfect atmosphere for a homicide scene. It had all the
elements: the victim's body whose remains are now dust, the
murder weapon, which is a sword that still had bloodstains, the
motive who called itself an entity that imitates a shadow but isn't
one, and last but not least, the offender; a man with no prior crime
who did not hesitate and committed his first one. To the
knowledge of Quetzalcoatl, everything must have gone according
to the bastard's plan. Even though he did not say much, he sent
Naran to be the vessel. There was nothing that he could do, and
deep down, he did not want to do anything to stop him. *Some
things are meant to come to an end.* Even with this thought in
mind, it still bothered him. Humans were stupid and useless,
mainly because they didn't value essential things. Is this reason
enough to end them?

For Quetzalcoatl being inside a human meant enjoying food,
water, feeling the rain; in other words, it meant being alive,
genuinely alive. He was able to see every part of the universe,
even the part of it that continued to move and expand; yet,
nothing compared to Earth, to what this place meant, and the

beings that lived here. Maybe it was the fact that it was the host to a variety of portals to different dimensions, which made it the epicenter of evil and good, or perhaps, it was because Quetzalcoatl was once human, many centuries ago for a brief moment. It was attractive to him how he needed nothing yet craved everything, and once he was inside Naran, every emotion expanded. He found himself with an enormous thirst that drove him to a river with crystalline freshwater. If he could compare one sensation to another, the thirst, in particular, felt, to him, like that time when flames had pierced his insides, breathing was pure agony. And then, just when he started to feel his end, the bastard had stopped, interrupting his torture and making Quetzalcoatl exhale in ecstasy. The memory vanished, leaving him with an itch in his brain that he couldn't scratch. It appeared satisfying his thirst would not happen today.

Gazing at the night sky, every planet and distant star spread before his eyes, with such unique colors, dancing to their song. Feeling his acquired body wrapped by the water as he floated, he kept admiring the great sky. For a moment, he forgot everything. For a moment, he was free, and that thought brought him back to his present. As he stepped out of the river, he could feel Naran, a reminder that the bastard had something in mind. *So, what if this is a trap, I had nothing up until now! Not even a physical form. This world... it's hard to let it go.* His thoughts were interrupted, yet again, by the voice of Naran shouting out his name.

"Ugh! What do you want?"

"You're slowing us down. The god gave us orders that we need to obey."

He was unaware of such accusations, and even if it was his doing it, it irritated him to be scolded. "Oh, I'm sorry! Wait, not true. That's your problem, not mine, and he does not order me around!"

He felt a sudden urge to leave Naran and continue to be an amorphous being of energy. *He has no idea what I have gone through for that bastard, yet, he wants me to help him with this stupid quest!* He thought, which made him angrier when Naran spoke again.

"But you said-"

"I only agreed to share my abilities. You now have strength, and other things, so I kept my end of the bargain!"

"The god said that you would help me."

And that retort finally set him off. "'The god said you would help me' Listen, human! I don't care about what that bastard says. We made a deal. I did my part, now leave me alone!"

Clinging to his last shred of sanity, Quetzalcoatl filled his mind with the image of a familiar female silhouette. For a moment, he felt his heart again. The thought of her made everything bearable, and at the same time, it helped him realize that nothing matters anymore. He even felt guilty being able to smell leaves or feel the water against his borrowed skin. *She would have loved this place,* he thought, as Naran kept walking through a road full of tall trees. Then a memory surfaced so clearly: he was near a tree holding her while the sun rose.

"You can see the sunrise later. Duty comes first." Naran's voice overpowered the memory, once again annoying Quetzalcoatl in the process. However, his irritation turns into curiosity when a foreign image appears before him. It was a memory that came from the human. After witnessing the memory, it became more apparent that someone whose spirit had been broken becomes the perfect vessel.

"So, is this why you became a coward?" Quetzalcoatl teased, which infuriated Naran

"That's none of your business!"

"Ooh, look who became feisty. Did I hit a nerve?"

"Enough!"

For the first time, Quetzalcoatl smiled. It was fun to forget about his problems and torture someone else.

Time runs differently for Quetzalcoatl, even if he is sharing a human body. It's as if time splits into two strands his, and Naran's, yet he can observe both. Other than that, they saw and felt the same. However, something kept bothering Quetzalcoatl. The first demon they encountered had not looked like the ones he remembered. The details of the creature did not add up.

The constant whining from Naran kept distracting him "oh please, would you relax!" he said and put back his attention on the demon. *There that would do.* It had been a couple of millenniums since the last time he saw a demon, so perhaps it could be that they had changed and evolved. As he continued to struggle trying to identify the unknown enemy, Naran came across another creature, and a sudden urge overpower both of them, "kill it already!" He said, a bit more desperate than he intended. *Why do I have this feeling of wrongdoing?* He couldn't focus on the emotion because he was distracted by the creature's body laying on the floor "remember to-"

"Yes, I know. Burn the body!" Naran's quick response made, for some reason, Quetzalcoatl feel proud.

"Relax! You won't get hurt," said Quetzalcoatl, trying to calm Naran's heart so that he could perform the new ability correctly. He reminded him of a little brother, someone you wanted to protect and try to make happy. He kept instructing Naran on how to control the flames to avoid a major catastrophe. As he watched the body burn, he noticed that the fire was not changing colors. *Could it be they are not demons, but something else?* A sudden sickness overpowered his entire body. *If not demons, then what was Naran killing? What am I helping to kill?* The questions only made him feel worse, and then the thought of Her finding out that he was helping to eliminate an entire species made his whole being dissipate for a second. *She is dead.* He thought, trying to comfort his nagging conscience.

History began overflowing Quetzalcoatl's mind; it was something he disliked doing, yet is the best way to solve this puzzle. When the demons started creating trouble on Earth, several entities interfered, trying to secure the safety of the human race, including him. For every monster he burned, he recalled, the flames turned from orange to violet. After putting a seal on the inferno, peace had returned to the Earth; that is until the supreme found out that the bastard Kinich Ahau, or the god, as Naran calls him, had been behind it all. *If the supreme hadn't been such a fraud, I would have been liberated by now, and She would still be with me.* The thought darkened his mood. It was the reason why he avoided thinking about the past at all costs. He told himself repeatedly that there was nothing he could have done to change things. That is how it was destined to be.

Thoughts kept swirling in Quetzalcoatl's mind. What species would, Kinich Ahau, have decided to camouflage so that Naran could not know—and him neither. As he feared that it might be humans, the pain began to fill his soul. Then Naran ran into a young human and commanded him to gather everyone in the fields that were far away from the altepetl, and he exhaled deeply, feeling alive again. *If they are not human, then what are they? I am not aware of any other species that exist alongside humans, especially one so vast. And why is Naran getting tired? It is nearly impossible for him to get fatigued now that I am inside of him.* While he pondered all of this, he kept noticing that the demons would not fight first; they simply stood there as if frozen. The more he focused on their eyes, the more he saw a pattern. *They are afraid.* Which means Naran was killing innocent beings. With that thought in mind, he tried to get him to see past the grotesque exterior of the creatures.

"Don't you think it's weird?"

"What's weird?"

"They don't attack you."

"That's because I'm quicker."

And with that, he realized that no matter what he said to him, Kinich Ahau had cast a deep spell. *And those are very hard to get rid of.* He acknowledged based on experience. Even knowing this, it didn't explain why he couldn't see the proper form of these beings. He saw the same awful creatures Naran was seeing. Why would Kinich Ahau go to that extent?

Furthermore, why did he request this from Naran if he could have killed all these creatures with a simple snap of his fingers himself? Her face appeared, cutting right through the middle of his questions. *If you had been in my position, you would have fought and not settled as I did.* This thought made him try once more, but it was useless. *He's gone now, which means Kinich Ahau's plan is much bigger than what I had anticipated.*

Continuing Naran's time frame

Chapter 5

Standing outside the chantli of Teotihuacan's Tecuhtli, Naran's chest kept rising and falling faster than usual for his new state. With the sword tip touching the floor and his hand barely able to hold the grip, it could easily pass as the protagonist of one of those legends he had heard when the brave hero stood still, with the weapon in his hand, dripping blood, exhausted after having saved the world. On the contrary, that was not how Naran felt now. There was something inside his head, something that made him feel anxious and disoriented.

He looked up at the sky, noticing the dark clouds surrounding him. "I have done what you asked of me," he said with a low and sorrowful voice. Drops of water began to land on his face. A sudden pressure on his chest appeared, followed by an enormous amount of pain, making him drop to his knees. Just when he felt death was near, a scream escaped his lips. *This was your choice, now deal with the consequences!* Quetzalcoatl said to him, and for the first time, Naran found comfort within this being's words, as if Quetzalcoatl could understand what he was feeling.

The rain began to put out the remaining flames on some of the bodies, as if wanting to cover up the massacre, trying to repair the damage, yet it was useless. The land became silent.

For many years Teotihuacan had been the most extensive and busiest altepetl of all. The one with a few more orders, a few more laws. Now, it was as if it had never existed.

Naran stood on a pond of blood under his feet, a mix of blood, water, and his tears. His clothes were hardly stained; yet, his soul had stains, many stains. The type of stains that will not come off no matter how many times you wash. His mind pulls him into a dark place, one that he had avoided for many years. A place that he chose to ignore but could not any longer; he was unable to forget, and as he watched the blood slowly drip from his hands and tasted it on his lips; knowing very well that the blood was not his; sanity slowly began leaving him.

"Good job!" The Sun appeared, but Naran didn't bother to look at him; he didn't wonder how, or when, or if he had seen everything.

His words only made Naran's heart shatter a little more. "Then why do I feel this way?" Naran's voice was weak and barely audible for the first time since he had met the Sun and Quetzalcoatl.

The Sun kneeled next to him, looked him in the eye, and said, "you saved everyone!"
Naran wanted to believe, wanted to hang on to those words, but the feeling of wrongdoing was the only thing that seemed genuine and truthful.

"You have done a magnificent job!" the Sun said again, grabbing Naran from the shoulders and slowly helping him up. The smile of the god made his insides twist; his mind went blank and drifted away into blessed nothingness.

Chapter 6

A cold breeze covered his body, and distant laughter echoed in the dark place. He tried to get up, feel the ground, and find some sort of support, but there was nothing. He couldn't tell if his eyes were open or closed. Then panic seized him, making him run. But, how could he know if he was escaping if there was no direction? He bent down, holding his knees on his chest, *Naran* a distant whisper said, he tried to respond and realized he had lost his voice. He was trapped inside the nothingness.

"This is what he does," the whisper turned into a voice, a male voice. Naran was unable to identify where exactly it was coming from. "He is not light, and you are just his pawn."

A figure began to form. However, only the eyes were not visible. Something about the figure was familiar to Naran. "You are broken" the voice became more evident, and the figure presented itself, and it looked just like Naran, except for the eyes. *Quetzalcoatl!* Naran thought.

"Precisely! my empty man." Naran stood still, watching Quetzalcoatl move around, observing the light particles trailing him as he walked. "I also wondered why he chose you. Now I know. You are empty. Every human has something to believe in, something to fight for, even if it's a small dream. You, on the other hand, lost everything when your mother died. If only she had died of natural causes." Naran tried to scream, wanting him to stop, yet Quetzalcoatl kept ignoring his tears, his pain. "Maybe things could have been different for you; however, it doesn't change the fact that your people killed her, the same people that ensured your safety. The same people that claim to be good and murder when there is a lack of rain. Oh, but it wasn't those people's fault, was it? Don't get me wrong. They were awful because it wasn't enough to kill your mother and forced you to watch. No, they gave you a tecpatl; they gave you a weapon and a choice, but the worst part was that you were too weak to use it to defend your mother." The memories came rushing back, and Naran lived everything once again, as he did every night in his nightmares. The pale face of his mother, her eyes full of fear, begging him to stop. He was given two options: he chose to save his own life and end hers. "You killed her without hesitation, just like you killed those creatures." He felt his mind shatter; felt every thought melting and burning under his skin; felt the guilt consuming him to his bones. "And you thought you could keep on going, pretending that it had been an order that you couldn't refuse."

Please stop! his lips moved, yet no sound came out. "You had a choice and made a decision."
Quetzalcoatl put his left hand on Naran's shoulder and rested the index finger of his right hand directly on his heart. "You. Are. Broken." Quetzalcoatl pushed his index finger with those final words, creating such pain and agony that Naran drifted away

once again.

Rambling thoughts kept Naran's mind spinning and in constant pain. He could not focus on the images that had been presented to him. He wondered if he was dead, alive, or asleep. After a few moments, or could have been decades, he caught the silhouette of a brunette woman with soft eyes and long black hair. *"Mother!"* He uttered involuntarily because the heart will never forget what his mind tried to forget. His mother smiled at him, making him feel she was really there. Tears began to appear in his eyes, and for the first time since that horrible day, he let everything out. *"I'm sorry!"* he sobbed. *"I'm sorry, mother!"* His heart broke again under her warm gaze, and it appeared as if she could hear him. *"I couldn't save you. I ended your life! I did!"* He brought his hand to his chest, trying to rip out his heart.

The only person who had loved him unconditionally, the woman who gave birth to him, who cooked his favorite meals, who tended his wounds with kisses and hugs, the only one who deserved to be happy was dead, by her own son's hand *"I...did!"*. She slowly began to dissipate into mist, Naran tried to grab her, to hold her hand, but it was useless. *"Forgive me!"* he cried as his mind sank into nothingness once more.

Chapter 7

The pain of sore muscles made him open his eyes, he tried to move, yet his legs did not respond. However, nothing compared to the pain in his chest; that was the worst of all. His mind was in chaos. Every time he tried focusing his vision on something, the result was a shapeless blur, making it harder to pinpoint where he was. The only thing that remained intact was his hearing. The sound of the wind rustling through leaves, the melody of birds, and the breathing of a person. "Who is there?"

"It's me, relax. Try to focus on my voice." The Sun's soothing voice calmed his heavy breathing. "I thought I lost you for a second." Immediately a sensation of safety and wellbeing covered his entire body; however, it only lasted a few moments. Without warning, images of the dead demons appeared in his vision. "Breath Naran, everything turned out great!" It seemed that the Sun knew the troubled thoughts Naran was having. He opened and closed his eyes several times. A sigh escaped his lips. *It was just a dream,* he thought.

"How do you feel?" The question forced Naran to return to the present. "You must have gone through a lot. For being your first quest, you did a fantastic job!" The images of the burning demons and blood everywhere returned, making him finally empty his stomach. "Ugh! You, humans, are disgusting!"

Quetzalcoatl had that same reaction. Dismissing the thought quickly and clearing his mouth, he tried to remember how he got to his chantli, but unable to recall, he finally asked, "What happened?"

"You fainted or died? Not sure. It seems my little pet did not do its job."

"Do you mean Quetzacoalt?"

The Sun tensed and turned, studying every movement Naran made, "so, he told you?"

"Tell me what? His name?"

"Just his name?" Asked the Sun, tension betraying his ordinarily cheerful demeanor.

"Yes."

And just like that, every muscle of the Sun's body relaxed. *It seems he is afraid of Quetzalcoatl.* For a moment, Naran's mind cleared, and he remembered his conversation with Quetzalcoatl. "He said I was your pawn."

The Sun laughed and kneeled, putting his hand on Naran's shoulder. He said, "ignore that thing. He is just part of me… well, the disgusting part anyway. You and I have more important things to do, and sleeping for a week is delaying my plans."

Though no one in history —to Naran's knowledge— had decided to go against the will of a god, after almost dying and remembering his poor mother, he had to try "I-I don't want to do this anymore."

"What!" The harsh voice matched the Sun's face-breaking

character again.

"I-I am done." Naran stood up, feeling dizzy.

The Sun blocked his path. "I don't think you understand..." He extended his hand towards a ray of light and began to manipulate and bend it as if it was an object. To Naran, it looked like he was creating an arrow similar to the shape he used on the Tecuhtli back in the Olmec altepetl "...I was not asking you." He took the lighting arrow and struck directly at Naran's chest, deleting all doubts, vanishing the images and memories of conversations with Quetzalcoatl.

Waking up with a nasty headache, Naran found the god sitting next to him, "what happened?"

"A powerful demon attacked you from behind. I came just in time." A fuzzy image of him falling to the ground, and one of those creatures attacking him with a tecpatl, surfaced in his mind as he slowly closed his eyes. Nevertheless, something felt out of place, as if this memory shouldn't belong in Naran's head, had he dreamed it? Carefully standing up with the help of the god, he slowly started to gain back his strength. They stepped out of the chantli and began to walk to some unknown place once again.

Something kept bothering Naran. He couldn't grasp what it was; he just knew there was something wrong. *Could it be that the demon attacked me with a curse that affected my mind?* he wondered. Dwelling on this matter only made his head feel worse.

"Are you ok? You are quiet."

He sounds so friendly, but there is just-

"Did you hear me?" The Sun interrupted his train of thought, forcing him into the present again.

"Yes, of course, I'm just in pain."

"Ah! Well, you almost died. So, it is perfectly normal." Naran simply nodded, not wanting to use his voice, fearing it would betray him, which he also noticed sounded different than what he remembered.

"I found that there is a large demon congregation on the Toltec altepetl; to be more precise, an army. Can you believe that?"

Naran stopped walking, feeling anxious and worried, "Why do they need an army?"

"They heard that someone was killing them. So, I guess the monsters feared they would not be able to defeat you."

"If one demon almost had, I can't imagine what a whole horde would do."

"That is why this time we are going to do things differently."

"What do you mean?"

The Sun turned and held Naran by the shoulders. "You need to pretend you are one of them," he let go of Naran as he continued; "on the borders of Tula, there is a small group of demons," he began pacing back and forth. "By the time you reach the altepetl, the demons will already have taken over. These demons are like no other I have seen. They can absorb humans and learn every aspect of their lives," said the god with exasperation. "So, I believe it will be safer for nearby altepetl if you supplant the demon's lord and try to control them."

"Lord?"

"It means Tecuhtli in your language," he stopped and turned to look at Naran, "don't get any funny ideas. These creatures will not show any mercy. Don't hesitate." Naran stood still, listening to the words coming out of the Sun's mouth. He knew they were important, but he could not make sense of them; his mind had begun wondering again. "The only thing they want is to get rid of any human" There were more instructions and details, but they just went right through Naran. *He seems different. There is no more light surrounding his body and his eyes; there is a bit of desperation, and-*

"Naran! I'm speaking to you of important matters" the Sun shook his shoulders, forcing him to dismiss all thoughts and worries. "Concentrate."

"Yes, yes, I heard you. Go to Tula and present myself as…."

Exasperation was all that the Sun gave Naran at that moment. "As the demon lord. He goes by the name Ce Acatl" the god chuckle, "this only proves how fast they are usurping human behavior. This is why you are going to take his place" he turns and, with a severe face, said, "this demon lord has created an army, and you are going to lead them to their doom."

"How can they have created an army if they-"

"It doesn't matter when or how!" The Sun took a moment to calm himself then continued, "what is important is that you go there, take Ce Acatl's place, and destroy them from the inside." Naran kept quiet, heard everything the Sun had to say, and followed him towards what he could imagine was Tula.

Chapter 8

There was no need to bother the Sun with his thoughts, but his thoughts kept creeping, and he could not avoid them. *How exactly did I get here? And all those creatures I killed, how was I able to do that? Something is missing, something important-*

"Naran"

It seemed every time he was about to discover some truth, the Sun interrupted. "Yes?"

"Let me tell you a story; my story, to be precise." Suddenly Naran became alert and moved closer to him, not wanting to miss a thing. "Many millennia ago, before any of your kind were born, this world was full of calmness, nature, and wilderness. It stood in perfect balance. I recall the sky being a richer color, and the scent of the air was the purest. My family, the people that I grew up with, decided that it was time to leave this world because soon, a new type of creature, similar to us, would appear. A few days after the news, I saw groups of humans appear out of nowhere, no, that would be a lie because they came from somewhere, but I could not tell from were exactly. We were instructed not to disturb your kind and to become invisible if we wanted to remain here.

"The things you eat, the dances, the way you behave, the need to believe in something higher, and the way your kind shows affection; it was all so different from everything I had ever seen. When the huentli began, the sacrifices, the pain, the tears, I couldn't help myself. I thought if I let them know that it's up to them, that there is no need for death, that they will be fine by just going back to that affection, that unique way of loving, everything will be alright. That was the first mistake I made. Once I made myself visible to them, I felt every beating heart, I felt all that need and desire, and I could no longer walk away. I had to stay.

"This one human, in particular, she was no ordinary woman. Never have I felt such things for another being, not even in my kind. I had broken so many rules just by showing myself; falling in love, a term I learned from your kind, would surely bring me death. And death is not painless; for us, death is a constant destruction of every particle in our body for the rest of eternity. I knew this, and yet, I still pursued this feeling.

"I wasn't the only one who was captivated by your kind. The difference was that he desired the love of every single human. He wanted to be the only one that received admiration; he didn't care for the sacrifices as long as they were made for him." The Sun stopped walking and sat on a texcalli, looking nostalgic by recounting the memory. Naran sat on the ground listening intently as if the Sun was a Teopixqui, someone who deserved his full attention. "The elders of our kind found out that there was someone promoting massacres and manipulating the humans; though, they were not sure of who it was. I kept silent because if I told them, he would tell them about me too, and I couldn't afford to lose her. So, I remained indifferent to the horrific events that unfolded upon your kind.

"She was the air that I needed to survive. I even discovered a way to be human, so I could see the world as she saw it; however, this cost me more than I could have ever imagined." He stopped and looked up at the sky. It seemed he was holding his tears. *He looks so vulnerable.* "He told me that all I needed to do was to create a distraction, a simple distraction, and once I did this, he would help me become human. I didn't care about the details. I just cared for her. I did as he told me, and just when I thought he would grant my wish, she found out what I did to become human. Let's just say that death was less painful than how I felt by how she looked at me. She turned away from me. He convinced her to turn me in. She decided to believe him, that bastard!" The Sun went silent, and to Naran's surprise, a tear rolled down his cheek. *I didn't know a god could cry.* He thought, and with all his heart, he wanted to believe the story.

"Cleansing the world from evil will make things right. She will be happy, and maybe she will forgive me. Wouldn't you do everything to be forgiven by the only person who loved you?"

Naran bit down the sudden pain that threatened to surface again, his regrets. He needed to believe that the words spoken by the Sun were genuine. "What happened after that?"

The Sun sighed and looked directly at Naran's eyes. "He made my story his. Anger is much more powerful than love, and I was able to trade my life for her; yet, this action bound us, made us part of each other."

"I don't understand. Who are you talking about?"

The Sun turned to Naran, looked him directly in the eyes, and said nothing for a few seconds; it appeared he was debating if he should continue or not. Then finally he said, "You met him... Quetzalcoatl." When Naran heard that name, everything came rushing back, and something inside of him broke into a million pieces.

He could not understand what exactly he was doing; meddling in a war between gods. He did not belong here. *This isn't my fight,* he thought, as he brought his hand to his chest. He felt his heart like a foreign organ that he had never used before as if this was the first time, he was experiencing what it was to have one.

"I'm done!" He screamed at the Sun's face and stood up to walk away.

"I know this might not feel right to you," the Sun said, which made Naran's anger rise.

"I don't care anymore! I'm done with you and Quetzalcoatl!" With that said, he started walking, kept moving forward, even though it was tough to do so.

"Do you know why I chose you?"

And that simple phrase made Naran fall to the ground, tears pouring out instantly. "I don't want to know," said Naran with a shaky small voice. *I don't care anymore. I want to die. Let me die already!* He begged even if it was only in his thoughts.

"Naran, humans are reborn. Did you know that?"

"What the fuck are you saying?!" For the first time since his mother died, he allowed himself to swear. Long ago, he had vowed not to curse as a way to honor his mother's memory, but right now, it didn't matter.

"The funny thing is, you always have the same eyes; that's how I'm able to find you, no matter how many times you are reborn. Your eyes stay the same. They are, after all, a reflection of your soul."

"Are you shitting me! I AM NOT HER!"
The Sun approached Naran kneeling in front of him, "let me show you."

"No!" he screamed, but the Sun did not listen. He grabbed Naran's head, and as he did, images of a young girl started to appear. Then they began to change, different people, different scenarios, and all of them had one thing in common, their eyes were the same; oddly, they seemed familiar to Naran. Also, for some unknown reason, the holders of such eyes get killed every time by a tragic event. None of them seemed ever to reach old age.

The images kept flashing, and the story the Sun had told unfolded in front of Naran's eyes. The last thing he saw was a rainy day in a field, and countless lifeless bodies lay at the feet of Quetzalcoatl, making Naran snap out of the daydream. "What did Quetzalcoatl do?" That was the only question that he needed an answer to.

"Now, do you believe me? Now, do you see who the real villain is?" said the Sun, not answering Naran's question. He could only imagine that Quetzalcoatl had slaughtered humans as Naran had killed an entire species; however, even after all this, something seemed off. "It doesn't make sense."

"Some things never do."

Stepping away from the Sun, trying to grasp air, Naran felt chaos churning within him. He felt as if he was trying to hold on to the edge of a cliff, knowing that if he let go, there would be no turning back. *What's the worst that could happen? I have killed my mother. It doesn't matter if in a past life I was someone else; in this one, I am a killer; an assassin hired to kill a bunch of pitiful creatures that I'm not sure are as bad as the Sun claims. I had blood on my hands even before this. There is no hope for me. Since the beginning of my existence in the female body, I have betrayed the person who loves me. None of us deserve to live, not the Sun, not Quetzalcoatl, and not me. Humanity will have been so peaceful without us. It's too late now, there is no turning back, and if I'm honest, I stopped caring about anything else the moment I took my poor mother's life.*

With all these thoughts toiling in his mind, turning his back to the Sun, Naran said, "For all I know, we are the villains. I don't care if I'm her or not. You want me to keep killing these supposed evil demons; fine, I will do it. And when the time comes, we will all fall." Dusting off his clothes and looking at the Sun with such an intense gaze of disgust that not even the god could bear. Naran said, "Up until now, everyone has had a say in my life; has manipulated me. According to you, in all my previous lives, I always get killed. I will do this for you, but nothing else. After that, I'm done!"

Chapter 9

Naran sneaks into the chantli of the Ce Acatl. This time, he is not bothered by the disgusting smell and appearance. He moves swiftly, puts his hands around the creature's head, and quickly kills it with an effortless twist. "Quetzalcoatl!" he calls with a grave voice, not caring if someone heard. "Show yourself!" He demands. He no longer feels shy. Nor a little boy worth nothing. Quetzalcoatl's shadowy figure slides from Naran's body into the ground and then transforms into someone with no lips. "I don't care if you heard the Sun or not. I don't care about what you want. You will follow my orders. Now let's bring this place to ashes!"

"What makes you so sure I will do what you say?"

"If the story I just heard it's true, and I am that woman, you owe me for manipulating me."

Quetzalcoatl lowered his gaze. It seemed to be feeling ashamed, making Naran hesitate for a moment.

"I need to look like that," he said, pointing to the lifeless body on the ground. Quetzalcoatl only nodded and disappeared inside Naran again.

The contact with the creatures was inevitable. However, Naran tried to delay it as much as possible. He began by avoiding leaving the chantli and started growling whenever a critter entered the chantli. He wanted to make sure they feared him. Not only did he have to pretend to be Ce Acatl —that name sounded familiar for some reason— he had to face the images of his past lives that kept repeating in his mind making it impossible to meet Quetzalcoatl at that moment. Maybe it was difficult because both of their stories involved losing someone, they loved due to their actions. The whole situation frustrated him. Something didn't seem right, especially with the eyes. If he was that person he saw in many lives, then why did those eyes seem familiar and foreign at the same time?

Quetzalcoatl's perspective

Chapter 10

Quetzalcoatl witnessed the life of Naran unfold in front of his eyes, starting with his childhood. He would get hurt while playing and search for his mother. She would comfort him with a kiss, or a 'there, there' that healed his wounds. Then the tragic moment when he took her life.

"You killed her without hesitation, just like you killed those creatures." Quetzalcoatl knew that his words wounded Naran deeply. However, it wasn't deep enough. Mixed emotions overtook him. He could not comprehend how someone who claimed to love a person could ignore that feeling altogether and end a life?

Please stop! Naran's lips moved, yet no sound came out.

"You had a choice and made a decision." Quetzalcoatl decided to take matters into his own hands and end Naran's life. "You. Are. Broken." With those final words, he stretches out his index finger, presses it against Naran's chest, puncturing his heart, and watches him slowly drift to his death.

He knew that the moment Naran's life ended, so would his; that he would become nothing, not even a shadow; just a voice carried by the wind, that no one would witness. Guilt began to appear. *I have killed innocent humans before; at least this time around, this human deserves it.* And with this thought, he shook the guilt away. However, deep inside, a part of him admonished that it was not up to him to decide who is worthy of being alive.

Quetzalcoatl never cared for anyone else's actions, and in a way, he saw himself in Naran. Following orders without considering the consequences, trying to save themselves at the expense of someone else, and in both cases, the women they loved, the only person who cared for them, died. This realization brought a darkness that consumed him and reduced him to nothing. The only emotions that remained were sadness and anger. Then troublesome thoughts began to appear. All those years, condemned to be with the same being that had destroyed his love, and all for what? To give humans a chance, the same humans who kill, not caring who it was? Nevertheless, who was he to pass judgment when he had also killed for his benefit.

The darkness and emptiness surrounding him began weighing him down. His end had arrived. At least this time around, it was by his hand. It did not even hurt compared to the first time. If only he had not acted rashly and tried enclosing Kinich Ahau with his being. It was pointless to think about the what-ifs; after all, there was no one to blame but himself. He had tried acting brave and tried being the hero, all to clear his conscience that he did not even know he possessed. He had succeeded in decreasing the power of Kinich Ahau, yet his sins were a weak spot, one that Kinich Ahau took advantage of to reduce him to a mere shadow. He thought again. *There is no point in remembering the past now,* as the pain began to turn into sorrow. Slowly his mind began to dissipate. Blackness was all that was left.

Slowly, out of the darkness, a small light started to shine in the distance. It grew closer and closer. And just as suddenly as it had ended, Quetzalcoatl began to exist again, to feel again. *What's happening?* He wondered as he heard the beat of Naran's heart.

"Do you think I was going to let you go that easily?" He heard the voice of Kinich Ahau, and he was sure he was not saying it to Naran. It was directed at him. "Quetzalcoatl you fool! You just condemned yourself." The words he utters contained anger tinged with a hint of anguish, making Quetzalcoatl wonder, why exactly had the human revived? Naran began to breathe again, and within seconds, he had his eyes wide open.

Was Quetzalcoatl the witness to the possibility that Kinich Ahau cared about someone else's life? 'How do you feel?' Kinich Ahau asked with such tenderness that even he could have believed that he was a good god. He listened to the conversation intently and felt that something was off, but he could not figure out what it was. *Quetzalcoatl had that same reaction,* 'he heard Naran's thought, and for a moment, a hint of hope began to form in Quetzalcoatl's head. Naran kept hiding essential details, and Kinich Ahau was buying it. Then all hopes died when Naran said, 'he said I was your pawn.' There was no use in trying to fight Kinich Ahau now. They had lost.

Not many divine relics had survived the first war, and the ones that had were hidden. Quetzalcoatl watched, horrified as the Lihtnao struck Naran. *How convenient that of all the relics that*

Kinich Ahau could have possessed, he had the one that was powerful enough to erase doubts and vanished memories, sealing them without a way to get them back. It meant the end for Quetzalcoatl. With sadness, he watched as Kinich Ahau brainwashed Naran, blocking any communication between them. *Maybe it was all for the best.* There was nothing Quetzalcoatl wanted from a human who was easily manipulated and was a constant reminder of his past mistakes.

Death was the only thing Quetzalcoatl thought he had control of, and now, as it turned out, he had failed at that too. He was condemned to watch the days pass before him and not do anything about it. Naran will continue doing what Kinich Ahau wants, killing those creatures that could be the remnants of an entire species. Nevertheless, why did he care? He was no different than Naran. He had also justified his actions with the love he had for a woman. They were made for each other. And both of them shared the inability to stand up to Kinich Ahau. He may not be able to end him; however, Quetzalcoatl knew that he had enough power to, at least, ruin Kinich Ahau's plans. Even in this weak form that he had been reduced to.

Every time he had built enough courage to do something, an image of his deceased lover crossed his mind and stopped him. *Why keep fighting if she is no longer alive? Why save humans, or even a single human, if the only one who is worth saving doesn't exist?* One thing was for sure, no entity of his kind would be able to bear the things he did and keep going as if everything was fine. He was different, or maybe he had changed for her, became more human? *I was human once, for a brief moment, and it got me nowhere!* He thought as the painful memory replayed before his eyes.

Light surrounded Quetzalcoatl again, which could only mean that Naran had started to wake up. Sadly, even if Naran's head was a mess, he was ready to attack whenever Kinich Ahau commanded. The one thing that Quetzalcoatl hated most about Kinich Ahau was that he always found a weakness, a personal trauma, something that he could use against his victims to keep them at bay. So, it was no surprise when he heard Kinich Ahau narrate Quetzalcoatl's life as his own. *It's not enough that you stole my body. Now you are going to steal my story as well?* He thought as he lay there floating on the emptiness, preparing to relive his past once more.

After everything he had gone through, he had begun to forget the feelings he had lived. He listened to Kinich Ahau recount and, masterfully, described every emotion and feeling long forgotten. Hearing what occurred millennia ago, pronounced out loud, made him feel like it had just happened the previous night. Every word became a dagger that went right through his heart, and once again, he was reminded he had one. Then Kinich Ahau finished the story, letting some tears fall, just as Quetzalcoatl did when he saw her lifeless body.

I thought you cared about me. For a moment, I believed that it hurt you to see me broken when she died. Clearly, I was delusional. Not sure if Kinich Ahau could hear him, but he needed to say those words, even if it was just internally.

Naran started to fall into the trap. Although it was all a true story, Kinich Ahau was not the victim; if anything, he was the mastermind that orchestrated it all.

"What happened after that?" Quetzalcoatl heard Naran ask and his tone of voice suggested a remote possibility that he was not trusting Kinich Ahau's version of events.

"He made my story his. Anger is much more powerful than love, and I was able to trade my life for her; yet, this action bound us, made us part of each other."

Liar! Screamed Quetzalcoatl feeling angry and useless. *How could he do this? What more does he want?*

"I don't understand. Who are you talking about?" Doubt began to form in Naran's head. *Could it be that there might be a chance after all?*

"You met him, Quetzalcoatl."

When Naran heard that name, the seal that confined the real memories vanished, breaking Naran in the process. Never had that happened before. Once someone uses Lihtnao, it is impossible to break the seal. Yet, here he was witnessing the chaos with delight because even if nothing happened, even if things kept going the same way, Naran was getting on Kinich Ahau's nerves and was making him lose his touch. *I'm glad this human survived.* The scene continued unfolding before his eyes. "I'm done!" Naran screamed at Kinich Ahau's face. A smile formed on Quetzalcoatl's non-existent lips. *It seems the human had guts.* He chuckled and fueled Naran's rage to make sure he would not back down now.

"I know this might not feel right to you,"

Who knew Kinich Ahau could beg.

"I don't care anymore! I'm done with you and Quetzalcoatl!" Although the anger was on the right level, a human was not strong enough to confront Kinich Ahau; and Quetzalcoatl was not who he used to be. All his power had been taken away, or more accurately, had been given away.

"Do you know why I chose you?"

The image of the lost mother appears wearing Naran. There is nothing Quetzalcoatl could do to ignite the anger again. *She is, after all, his weakest point.* "I don't want to know." The hurt in Naran's voice brought memories that Quetzalcoatl tried so hard to forget. Then he heard his own words echoed in Naran's thoughts *'I don't care anymore, I want to die. Let me die already!'* Maybe they were not that different from humans,

"Naran, humans are reborn. Do you understand that?" Suddenly everything inside of Quetzalcoatl matched Naran. A sick feeling began to form on both.

"What the fuck are you saying!"

Yes, precisely! What exactly are you implying?

"The funny thing is, you always have the same eyes; that's how I'm able to find you, no matter how many times you are reborn. Your eyes stay the same. They are, after all, a reflection of your soul."

Everything went quiet inside his head. For a long time after Quetzalcoatl lost Her, there were so many things he wanted to say to Her. So many things he had to explain. The pain of not being able to do so had weakened his sanity. *This has to be a lie.* It is a specific type of pain, so strong that it did not shed blood or had injuries; this kind of pain absorbs you, brings you death; and then revives you; only to keep killing you in a vicious cycle. That was what Quetzalcoatl was experiencing.

"Let me show you."

No, please don't. He begged, knowing very well what was about to happen. Kinich Ahau grabbed Naran, and Quetzalcoatl froze. Images, thousands of them showing those beautiful eyes that had captivated him since day one. The eyes that had the power to pierce to his very core and made him believe he had a soul. The last time he had seen those eyes, they were full of hate and disgust, and now, there they were, full of life again. This reminded him, yet again, that it had been he who had taken the light out of those eyes. *If it weren't for Kinich Ahau, she would have remained dead.* A part of him tried to make an excuse and tried to find a flaw in what he was seeing, but the more he thought, the more it made sense of why he had chosen Naran as the vessel. It was a way to force total submission from Quetzalcoatl. Every desire to fight him died down with the last memory where lifeless bodies surrounded him. He tried to look away; yet, it was useless.

"What did Quetzalcoatl do?" Naran asked, bringing Quetzalcoatl into tears.

"Now, do you believe me? Now, do you see who the real villain is?"

I am not the villain, please. He knew I wanted to be with you, so he tricked me. I love you more than anything. You were not supposed to be there! Please believe me. But his voice got lost in Naran's thoughts.

"It doesn't make sense."

Yes, please! Don't believe him!

"Some things never do."

As much as Quetzalcoatl wanted Naran to refute every word Kinich Ahau had said, the fact remained that a couple of hours before, he had killed her —or tried to. *How could I not see it? How could I not feel her? We were one.* No matter how much he questioned, it would not change what he had done. He could not go back in time; he had tried several times.

From the moment he had met Naran, he had felt something strange. The pull he had felt. It could not all be a coincidence. *This must have been the grand plan Kinich Ahau had from the beginning. This was why he decided to put me in a tzatetl, a human relic.*

"For all I know, we are the villains. I don't care if I'm Her or not. You want me to keep killing these supposed evil demons; fine, I will do it. And when the time comes, we will all fall." A strong wave of heat enclosed Quetzalcoatl, and an unfamiliar sensation overtook him. He felt his essence consumed to the point of weakness. *Could it be that Naran had been able to take a piece of my soul? This could change everything.* They would no longer be in control, not Kinich Ahau, and certainly not Quetzalcoatl. For the first time in his life, he was experiencing fear. If Kinich Ahau found out that Quetzalcoatl might disappear in Naran's body, he would most likely dispose of Naran. *If she keeps reacting with this strong aura, it will make him wary. There must be a way to make sure she stays alive this time.* His thoughts became mute when he heard his name.

"Quetzalcoatl!" A thousand reasons to remain inside came to Quetzalcoatl. *I can't see her, not yet.* "Show yourself!" His efforts were futile, the command was too strong, and he was too weak to disobey.

"I don't care if you heard the Sun or not. I don't care about what you want. You will follow my orders. Now let's bring this place to ashes!" *She doesn't have to know the things I did long ago.* With that thought in mind, he acted like his usual arrogant self.

"What makes you so sure I will do what you say?"

"If the story I just heard it's true, and I am that woman, you owe me for manipulating me." *That's not the only reason I should do as you say,* Quetzalcoatl thought with sadness as he remembered the moment when he tried to end Naran's life just a while ago. "I need to look like that." He obeyed, unaware of what had happened and did not want to know how they got to that chantli. *She is becoming what she hated the most, and it's all my fault.*

Continuing Naran's time frame

Chapter 11

One of the creatures abruptly entered the chantli. Naran
instantly grabbed his sword and pointed it. The creature ignoring
Naran's action started to express that 'several children had gone
missing' with a tone of fear and sadness. Naran dropped the
sword, petrified by what he just heard. *This thing talks like a
human,* and just to make sure Naran had heard correctly, the
creature vowed in respect and shouted. "Protect us Ce Acatl
Topiltzin Quetzalcoatl"

"Who?"

The creature looked up to him in confusion, not sure of what
Naran meant. "You are our Prince One-Reed Feathered Serpent."
This only made things more confusing to Naran because the
terms this creature used were human, just like him, just like his
altepetl. The reference to the feathered Serpent and how he
vowed when calling him Quetzalcoatl made Naran suspicious
about everything the Sun had said to him. There was one way he
could think of, to learn the truth.

"Bring your Teopixqui," he ordered.

The creature opened and closed his mouth several times, clearly
confused; then, he responded fearfully, "you are our Teopixqui."

Sitting down slowly, his mind going blank, a tremendous

feeling of uneasiness overpowered him. In a split second, a million possibilities crossed his mind. In those possibilities, the thought of killing his own kind, his own people without mercy, the same way he had killed his mother, was the worst.

Could it be that after everything he had done to become a better person, to try and redeem his past actions, he had done completely the opposite? Had he really been so oblivious to the possibility that maybe this Sun was not a good god? He had heard about these gods at the Mayan altepetl. They refer to them as the dual gods because, according to the Mayan elders, the nature of your actions would determine the reaction of the gods. This meant that if you did something wrong, they unleashed their fury upon you, and vice versa. Most of the time, each god always carries an opposite meaning. By this rule, for every good god, there had to be a bad one. This information only added more conflict. *Why then, in the first battle, did the bodies stitch back together in strange ways? No human does that. I had to burn them to prevent this. Was it a trick? And, why would a god need me to kill people when they simply could erase the entire humankind themselves? Is it only because I am her? or maybe he is unable to hurt humans, so he needs someone to do it for him? is it possible that-*

"Ce Acatl"

Naran looked at the creature, whose looks did not resemble a human being. *Why do they look like that? Is this also a trick?*

"The children, please."

Naran's heart sank as he remembered that he had been killing tiny creatures for the past couple of days. Then he tossed their remains that did not turn into ashes in a cenote. *They were not demons!* With that thought burning in his mind, he dismissed the not creature and ran towards the cenote. *Maybe I can still save them,* but it was futile. No matter how much he desired to bring them back to life, they were gone forever.

Madness is the only word to describe what Naran was doing. He jumped into the cenote, submerged, swimming to reach the bottom, trying to find the remaining bones. The rest of the children had turned into ashes, so even in his madness, he knew there was no hope for them. The sense of guilt overtook his entire body, his mind drifting into darkness, yet again. *That's why they were so easy to kill,* he thought as he remembered their screams. *They were innocent souls, and I slaughtered them!* His tears were unnoticeable as they were consumed by the blue water around him.

He remained underwater, wishing for death to come, only to realize that it was because he no longer needed air to survive. Hours passed by, unsure of what to do next —now that death was no longer an option—, he took the few bones he had managed to find and swam to the surface. He laid them in the ground, and as he stared at the bones, his heart made grief incarnate, a thought crossed his mind.

"Quetzalcoatl!" he screamed, his heart pounding. *Please, let it be possible!* The shadowy figure appeared before him, and Naran did what he swore he would never do again. He kneeled, put his head on the ground as the praying huentli established, and begged with all his heart.

"Please bring them back."

"I can't."

"Please, I will do anything you ask." Quetzalcoatl bent down, and the way he looked at Naran made him burst into tears. They both knew it was impossible. What hurt Naran the most was that part of him had known. Quetzalcoatl tried to warn him a few times, but the only one he cared about was himself and the Sun. "Why didn't you stop me!" He screamed at Quetzalcoatl, "why did you let me do this if you knew?" He cried, trying to put some of the guilt on someone else.

"Because I wasn't sure either," Quetzalcoatl's words gave him some comfort. It meant he was not alone in this; they shared the tragedy.

Slowly Naran's heart calmed, and the tears ceased. He buried the bones and prayed to the unknown because the gods he had been taught to pray to were not worthy of devotion.

Naran had to atone for his actions. Doing his job as the leader of the Toltec altepetl —of what remained of it anyways— would not be enough. Children are the most precious life, the purest and innocent beings, and he had murdered them. He kept wondering about the pain they must have felt; if they had suffered long or died instantly. He knew that most of them had agonized under the flames. He could vividly recall their crying.

"Teopixqui, we are ready, sir," the servant who had been delivering all the information to Naran waited for him outside. He kept silent, trying to hold his tears in and his screams in his throat. Walking to the teôcalli, the sorrow weighed heavily on him. *I can't do this for much longer,* he thought and sat down where the servant instructed.

He knew these so-called demons were actually humans, but he couldn't avoid not seeing them as disturbing creatures. Not sure what would happen and submerged in his own dark thoughts, people began to gather around him. Then a woman with white robes walked with an armed man approaching Naran.

"What is this?"

"It's the huentli."

They handed him the tecpatl while the woman was placed on chakmoli. Naran stood up abruptly, tightening his grip. He kept looking at the chest of the woman, remembering what he had done a few years back.

"The head is what we need," the servant explained, thinking that Naran was aiming for the heart.

"Why the head?"

"tzompantli is our offering to the Ancient Gods." Naran's anger resurfaced. He had been mourning the children's death since the minute he found out the truth, and here he was, holding a tecpatl to end a woman's life, as a request from his own kind. Some of those children he had killed may have died anyway when they reached the sacrificial age.

His anger and sorrow turned into fury, and this overwhelmed him. *They don't deserve to live,* he thought as he decapitated the girl before him. It was the cleanest and quickest cut he had ever done, as if that's any consolation. Then the servant instructed him to take the head and place it in the tzompantli. He was born in a lower class, and it never occurred to him to learn of the traditions and rituals the upper level has to do. Thankfully the servant didn't suspect anything and helped him when he seemed lost. However, once he was there, they expected him to say prayers for the gods. To avoid any suspicion, he retired to his chantli, leaving Tezcatlipoca, his second in command in charge.

Life was not fair, and even if death came, he would reincarnate again and again. He had not asked for any of this. Any person who experienced the torture of living, killing, and dying, just to repeat it over and over again, would eventually go mad. It's heartbreaking to find out that life is so useless. There is no purpose. Even if he was born a Tecuhtli, Teopixqui, or a warrior, his hands would be covered by blood because it's either kill or be killed. That was the society he was born in, and apparently, for many centuries, had been the same.

Chapter 12

Every night Naran's head became a whirlwind of thoughts, making it impossible to sleep. Thinking got him nowhere, he had to do something, he had to find the truth, the question was how? If he asked Quetzalcoatl, it might alert the Sun, and he was not ready to face him. So, the only possibility that he found was asking for help from a real Teopixqui of another altepetl. Anyone would know more about gods than Naran. After thinking about which altepetl to approach and unsure where the Sun was precisely, he decided to go back to his own. Changing back to himself, to avoid raising suspicion among Ce Acatl's people, he traveled during the night, making the trip longer than usual. *It's stupid to believe he won't found out, but I have to try,* he thought, avoiding speaking out loud for the same reason.

The Olmec altepetl was deserted as he arrived. He located the Tecuhtli, and to Naran's surprise, he also looked like the creatures he was told were demons. This confirmed that the Sun had done something to Naran so he would not find a resemblance to his own kind.

"Who is there?" Said the Tecuhtli as Naran entered the chantli.

It seemed that he was unable to focus his eyes on Naran. As he watched his former Tecuhtli, desperation started to show. *There has to be a way to fix my eyesight,* he thought.

"It's Naran, remember me?"

"Come closer" Naran approached the man who was sitting on the floor. He began to touch Naran's hands then moved to his face in such a manner that made it clear he was blind. "I am sorry, but I'm unable to recall who you are."

"What happened to you?"

"Ah, it seems you are an outsider."

Naran tried closing and opening his eyes, rubbing them, and even punching his own head; yet, he still saw his Tecuhtli in a decrepit way. Nevertheless, he was still able to detect the sorrow in the poor man's voice as he said, "the wrath of the gods has been unleashed upon us."

Naran dreaded, for a moment, the possibility that this was all his fault; that perhaps, the Sun took away his eyesight. Trying not to be obvious, he asked, "Why? Where are all the people?"

The Tecuhtli became silent, and Naran feared the worst. "Most of them fled to Teotihuacan." A tear, threatening to fall, forced the Tecuhtli to stop and clear his throat, "as soon as they arrived, that altepetl also went down. I should have died with them, but I'm old, and I thought I was going to slow them down, so I decided to stay." He could not help it any longer, and tears began to fall as he recounted the events. "A light that resembled the sun, no! It was brighter than the sun, struck in the middle of the teôcalli. I got lucky and only lost my eyesight...others lost their lives. I can only assume they were too close to where the light hit." He composed himself and continued, "I thought it was temporary blindness. Time passed, and I stayed the same." More tears reached the ground, although this time they were from Naran as he recalled the fire he had caused. *There was a human. He reached out to me! I instructed him to gather everyone on the fields.* He thought, trying to make sense of all the mess.

"If only we had done the huntli on time, this wouldn't have happened."

Naran cleaned his face and bent down to be at the same level as the Tecuhtli. "What do you mean? I remember the preparations were going according to plan."

Tecuhtli denied with his head, "It was my fault. Everything was going perfect, and in a split of a second, I was found on the floor unconscious. When I woke up, I couldn't remember my name and to my surprise, five days had passed. It was naive of me to think that the gods would understand."

Naran rested his hand on Tecuhtli's shoulder. *In a way, this was also my fault.*

"I wonder what the Teotihuacan people did to deserve such devastation? Is it possible that it was because of us?"

"No, Tecuhtli, I don't think the events are related." Naran tightening his jaw. Lying had become as natural as breathing. Remembering why he was there in the first place, Naran cleared his mind and tried to lock down all the guilt and sadness away, even if it was only temporary. "A woman by the name of Xpiayoc used to live here. I was hoping you could tell me something about her."

The old man kept quiet. It seemed he was going through

his memories, trying to pinpoint the woman. "Ah yes, yes, I remember her now. She was a strange one."

"What do you mean?"

"We found her when she was a child, we never learned anything about her parents, I assume she was from another altepetl. She didn't speak for years." Tecuhtli smiled with fondness at the memory. "Once she started, no one could stop her. She always did what she was told and was well behaved. I raised her as my own daughter until that day."

Naran sat closer to the man, "what day?"

"She got pregnant with the seed from a slave. I wanted that child dead. She claimed she had been praying to the great Feathered Serpent to be gifted with a child." Tecuhtli's eyes took on a certain nostalgia and sadness. "If it was a gift from a god, then there was nothing I could do."

The casual reference to the serpent meant that Quetzacoatl was very well known among their people. However, it did not explain how exactly they knew him.

The image of his poor mother surfaced in Naran's mind threatening to break him. Instead, he forced down the tears and asked, "Do you remember the child?"

The Tecuhtli was silent for a few minutes, "I... can't remember."

It made sense that he did not remember him. However, he indeed remembered his mother, "and Xpiayoc. Do you know what happened to her?" He asked anxiously.

"I'm afraid I don't. My mind did not heal properly." And with those final words, every hope that Naran built suddenly died.

He could try and find someone, but it seemed there was no one left. "Is someone taking care of you?"

The old man smiled brightly, "yes, people come and go often." Naran laid his hand again on Tecuhtli's shoulder before leaving.

Pacing back and forth outside the altepetl, thinking there was no point in asking the Tecuhtli again. The night was approaching, and he should head back; he had been absent long enough, and it might raise suspicions. It never occurred to him to run. He never had to since he had started working. With that thought in mind, he took a deep breath and began running. After some time, he noticed he could keep running and not get tired. This motivated him to speed up. Guess this is also part of the so-called gifts Quetzalcoatl had given him.

Chapter 13

Finding the truth became a priority, whereas compassion and humanity came in last. This helped eliminate the guilt as he continued the sacrifices, executing up to three people per week, and one of those three people, more often than not, was a young girl. However, the truth was put to rest when a Zapotec princess named Xilavela showed up, saying she wanted to form an alliance between the altepetl. To Naran's surprise, she was the only one whose appearance was human and radiant nonetheless. This meant that she was an imposter. What kept Naran on edge was that he had seen this face before. Images of the day that the Teotihuacan altepetl ceased to exist —thanks to him— started to flash inside his head, and then it hit him. *She looks like the human I talked to that day.*

"The gods will punish us," Tezcatlipoca said, bringing Naran back to the present. It became a routine after each sacrifice to see Tezcatlipoca in his chambers. He started approaching in the teôcalli, and soon after, in Naran's chantli. Naran knew that the reason behind Tezcatlipoca's urge for more sacrifice was a strike. He wanted the power and position Naran had, and quite frankly, if Naran could, he would give it away on a silver platter.

"Is Xilavela still around?" Naran asked, focusing on his personal problems.

"That is not what we were discussing."

Patience was another thing Naran lacked lately. "Alright, I will make an announcement. Gather everyone at the teôcalli," said Naran dismissing Tezcatlipoca, who left with a smile, thinking he finally had agreed with him, when in reality Naran had other things in mind.

Replaying in his head the conversation Naran had with Tecuhtli, it occurred to Naran that the only way to know if these god's events had something to do with his mother's prayers, he had to ask the only god he had available, "Quetzalcoatl." The shadowy figure appeared before him. It had been a long time since they saw each other, mostly because he didn't know who to trust any more, and because he wasn't sure how involved Quetzalcoatl was with the Sun's plans; yet, he had to take the risk. "I have a question." Quetzalcoatl stood still, waiting for Naran to continue "What's the real name of the Sun?" Even though the shadow didn't have any face, it seemed to Naran that he was surprised, meaning he was on the right track. So, he continued, "my kind knows about you. Otherwise, they wouldn't call me Ce Acatl Quetzalcoatl. That name was given to you by us isn't it?" Naran paused for a second to get up and face Quetzalcoatl, then continued, "I have debated this matter for days. Kept thinking that it was unreasonable to see it as a coincidence that there is a mention of you on most of the altepetl. As I recall, when we first met, you were a feathered serpent. In my altepetl we spoke about a god that, if the woman prayed and gave offers to this god, they would conceive a child. What's most interesting is that my mother prayed to you to have me, or at least that's what Tecuhtli said to me." He paused talking to let the information sink in, but even if it was a breakthrough, this would only create more questions. "I will ask you again, what is-"

"Kinich Ahau," said Quetzalcoatl quickly without hesitation.

"The Eye of the Sun. Makes sense." said Naran thinking that he had a new lead. These so call gods have been seen by humans long enough for them to come up with names that resemble their appearance

"What will you do now?"

I ask myself that same question Naran thought as he smiled with confidence. "In a way, we are one. It's pointless to tell you if you are going to end up seeing it for yourself," he said as he left the chantli, not worrying if Quetzalcoatl went back into his body or stayed there.

Reaching the teôcalli where everyone waited, he spotted her. She was easy to find among all the disturbing appearances. This only created more questions, for example, why was Kinich Ahau letting Naran know the difference.

Focusing on the task at hand, he positioned himself facing the crowd. "I, Ce Acatl Topiltzin Quetzalcoatl, declare that the sacrifices should no longer be performed," he said with a strong voice. "That's all. Everyone, go back to your duties." Knowing the consequences and completely ignoring the shouting of disapproval —from some— he turned and left. This was no act of bravery, but of humanity. When his mother died, he stopped believing that sacrifices were a way to be on the good side of the gods because no worthy god would ever ask for blood, and so far, the gods he had met were useless, incompetent, and selfish. That made them more human than divine.

"You doom us all Ce Acatl, this will be punished by the gods. Two altepetl no longer exist. Why do you think that is? huh, look at me!"

Tezcatlipoca's rage made Naran pause. "Remember your position," he said without turning. "If what you say turns out to be correct, then you would have me to blame," and then he kept walking towards his chantli, hoping that Xilavela would approach him after this. After all, it was a message directly to 'him.'

Waiting patiently in his chantli, sitting in some sort of icpalli that was not there earlier, sat the princess waiting for Naran. "Well, well, look at you making a revolution. You know, it's the first time I see someone so powerless step up and try to undo a wrong." Even his voice sounded female-like.

"Aren't you angry?" asked Naran with a smile.

"Oh Naran, why on earth would I be angry?" Kinich Ahau approached him resting his arm on Naran's shoulder. "It's a hassle having to change appearance. So, I hope you don't mind if I stay like this." Naran watched Kinich Ahau's movements, thinking of how unsettling it was to see him so joyful "Sit Naran. I assume you have some questions." A chair appeared right in front of the icpalli. *Does this mean he already knows?* Thought Naran as he sat down. Smiling and waiting for Naran, Quetzalcoatl decided to join in the conversation.

"You're a motherfucking bastard! How could you?"

"Now, now Quetzal, watch your language. There is a human

present." Kinich Ahau chuckled at his comment while Naran stood still, unsure what would happen with two gods in an enclosed environment.

"What more did you want from her? isn't it enough?" said Quetzal with such mournfulness, showing how tired and hurt he was

Kinich Ahau's expression turned from pleasure to annoyance. "You know, I like you more when you are raging in anger. It's more fun that way," he said so casually, making Quetzal and Naran feel disgusted.

"Is this all a joke to you?"

"Yes, it is" he smiled again, making Naran's insights boil in anger.

"Is my mother dying a joke to you! Are all those innocent children dying a joke to you!" said Naran with his heart burning in sadness.

The eyes of Kinich Ahau rest on Naran. "Let me tell you a little secret. Do you know why they have that disgusting look? It's very simple. That's who they really are."

"That's the most absurd thing I have ever heard."

"Naran, despite what you want to believe, humans are disgusting beings. You have seen the sacrifices, the destruction of nature, the classes and ranks. You even have slaves!"

"And you are a selfish god who has destroyed an entire altepetl, so I don't see any difference."

The laughter of Kinich Ahau resonated everywhere, making Quetzal stand closer to Naran in a protective way. *Doubt he could do anything.*

"I can't disagree with you on that. Let me simplify what you are seeing is all the bad things that people have done and not only in this life."

"What about the children or the newborns?"

"Didn't you hear me? Those infants were adults once, and they will become adults later. You are seeing the ugly side of everyone's past, present, and future actions. Isn't it wonderful?" he clapped his hands in excitement. *So, this is who he really is,* Naran thought, feeling disturbed and uneasy by the so-called 'little secret,' "oh wait, that's not the secret." Naran could feel Quetzal tensing next to him. "This wasn't my doing," he smiles brightly as he looks at Quetzal.

Naran stood up quickly, stepping away from him. "So, you were working with him this whole time?" said Naran indignantly.

"That's not true, listen to me, he is lying-" Quetzal began to defend himself, yet the laughter of Kinich Ahau interrupted him.

"How about we stop blaming others and assume our responsibility," everything became quiet. For a moment, Naran felt that this was going to be the end. "Didn't you find out that your kind gave us the name we possess?" said Kinich Ahau with a calm and relaxed voice that matched his posture, reminding Naran of what mattered the most. "We were forbidden to interact with humans, and most of us ended up breaking the rule. Do you want to know why we were forbidden?" At this point, even Quetzal became interested. "Because your realm was not meant to hold us in it, so as soon as we enter it, we develop gifts as a side effect." He pointed at the shadowy figure. "For instance, Quetzal was seen by humans like the wind and life itself, which led them to believe that he had the power to make the infertile fertile. But he also gained the opposite. If it gave life, it could also take it away. Or in the case of the wind, which has nothing to do with air but with visibility. The opposite of this would be to see beyond the physical matter." Kinich Ahau paused, letting the information sink in. "Do you see what I'm getting at?"

"If I'm inside of Naran, then he can see how the people really are? that's ridiculous!" said Quetzal with disbelief

"Not who they are; rather, what they are, based on their actions. I know, I know, it's complicated. However, this, Quetzal, makes you responsible for the life *she* has endured. What would you do about it?"

Watching the shadowy figure walking around making gestures in exasperation was a first for Naran, and he could relate to what it may be feeling. His brain kept asking over and over, how could this be possible? Nevertheless, he had seen a god land; he had seen the rays of sun being manipulated as an object; a god lives inside him; and he experienced abilities that no human could have. So, even though it was an extraordinary, and hard to believe, piece of information; it made sense. "Why are you telling me this?" Naran asked without looking directly at Kinich Ahau because part of him feared that his brain would break more than it already was.

"You can think of this as a moment of weakness, and Quetzal, you can see it as torture." The laughter resonated all around, almost as if they were in a cave.

"Is this why you came?"

"I wanted to check on you to see how you were doing.

However, that speech you gave in the morning was...thrilling."

And then the words Kinich Ahau had said came back to Naran: *'most of us.'* "How many of you are among us?" he asked. The questions that Naran was asking made Kinich Ahau smile with a hint of pride. "Look Quetzal, he is cleverer than you," he mocked, again and moved his body so that he would be closer to Naran, "more than you can imagine."

"Wouldn't that ruin your plans?" Quetzal said, making Kinich Ahau break eye contact with Naran to look at him now.

"The thing is, most of them don't remember who they really are, so no harm done." He stood up and walked around the room. If it was unnatural to see him as a male, seeing him as a female was disturbing. "I will be leaving soon. You can ask whomever you want and gather all the information you'd like, and when you are ready, I will be waiting." He then turned to Quetzal and said "Ah and don't worry, my plans will keep going unaffected." Before leaving he caressed Naran's cheek, leaving behind a tingling sensation that lasted for a few minutes. "I knew you'd turn out to be perfect," he whispered in Naran's ear, which made him feel strange.

"Leave!" Quetzal yelled, startling Naran and making Kinich Ahau laugh one last time before disappearing.

Left alone and unsure of what to do, Naran and Quetzal avoided each other. Unable to dismiss what Kinich Ahau had said and knowing that it made perfect sense it also made everything a bit more complicated for Naran.

Quetzal went back to being the monotonous shadow figure he always had been, although he kept showing signs of indignation, which piqued Naran's curiosity. "Why are you angry if you are just like him?"

"I tried to change."

Naran went silent and sat down on the icpalli that Kinich Ahau had left behind. "That's the problem. How can you change what you are? The moment you entered my body, I started to see humans as creatures, and you did that without even knowing."

"Are you going to believe him? He lies! That's what he is good at, lying and misleading everything and everyone!"

"Who gave you the name of Quetzalcoatl?"

"That doesn't prove anything."

"And if we find another god, will that convince you?"

The shadowy figure lay on the floor defeated, "If we do that, it would only endanger you further." And with that, Naran realized that Quetzal hadn't done this on purpose; that he also was in a trap; and that he was trying to do the best he could now that they both knew who Naran really was.

"I am not her, at least not in this life. I would appreciate it if you could save your sentiment."

Quetzal sat up, getting closer to Naran, which made him recoil "Then let me see you as a brother that I have to protect." It seemed that he was begging, and Naran was too tired to care.

"Then find a way for me to stop seeing the sins of people." Even if he meant what he said, it actually didn't bother him anymore. After seeing Kinich Ahau as a human, he kept thinking that it could be an advantage. Nevertheless, after hearing why this happened, it hurt him to see his reflection altered by his sin.

It was not easy for Naran to comprehend Kinich Ahau's information, mainly because he actually killed innocent people and kept on doing so. He is marked by his actions. Not only is he a murderer, but he is also one by choice. He kept thinking about his early justification for what he had done: that a god would never make him commit such atrocities. Clearly, he was wrong. The problem was that he saw the warnings; nonetheless, he was so empty and hurt that he desperately wanted to fill the void with the light Kinich Ahau provided, not bothered to wonder where it came from. Looking at Quetzal that had started to blend in with the darkness of the chantli, he came to agree on one thing with Kinich Ahau: he should stop blaming others and assume his responsibility. Crying or feeling sorry for the lives he took would not bring them back. *What is important now is to investigate, and to do so, I need to leave this place.* He was aware that there were many unanswered questions, and he couldn't just keep assuming or hoping for the best.

Chapter 14

This was a journey with multiple paths, and Naran had to choose carefully. One wrong turn and he could fall right on Kinich Ahau's trap.

For instance, he could do several things: go back to his altepetl and help Tecuhtli regain his memory. Leave toward the Zapotec altepetl where he could find a Teopixqui that could answer some questions from their current princess. One thing was sure: he had to depart from the Toltec altepetl doesn't matter if, since his last speech, everything had turned upside down. He didn't regret it because it was the first step towards change.

If he could establish this new rule, he would prove wrong what Kinich Ahau said about humans' inability to improve. Tezcatlipoca is the only obstacle standing in Naran's way. He had started raids, convincing people that Naran was a demon sent to destroy them. They had created plans to trap and kill him as an offer to the gods. Naran tried several times to change people's minds, yet it was hard to do so when that's all they had known their entire lives. He had thought that if he pretended to be a god, maybe they would listen. Yet, when he showed off some of his abilities, Tezcatlipoca interrupted, saying Naran was an evil spirit, which made it reckless to show Quetzal at that point.

Thinking what to do was time-consuming, and the longer he stayed there, the more it would probably benefit Kinich Ahau's plans. Decisions needed to be made. However, Naran's guilt made it challenging to leave Tula in the hands of Tezcatlipoca. Knowing the truth made him feel responsible for their well-being. Also, abandoning Tula reminded Naran of all the times he had turned his back on everything due to his desperate need for love. That same necessity drove him to do unspeakable things.

Nonetheless, his presence here was useless. *If we are supposed to die, then what if I stay and we die together. There is no guarantee that I will stop Kinich Ahau, but I can try and make everyone's deaths less painful.*

"I finally found a way to destroy you."

A voice interrupted Naran's thoughts, making him face the intruder. "I have no time for you, Tezcatlipoca."

"Yes, you do, Naran." The astonishment in Naran's face gave away everything that Tezcatlipoca wanted to know. "It took me a while to figure out your true identity." He smiled victoriously, "after seeing your display of unnatural actions and your disapproval of our traditions, I only had to connect the dots."

Naran kept silent. *There is no way he could have known* "I see right through you" then, behind him, a shadowy figure appeared, making Naran believe that Quetzal was the one who helped him. "Aren't you curious to know?" Tezcatlipoca continued talking with a cocky tone, yet Naran was busy looking at Quetzal, trying to find out if he was doing this.

"I assume you will let me know."

Tezcatlipoca laughed, and suddenly, his appearance became

human, shocking Naran. "What?" said Tezcatlipoca. *It seems he is not aware.*

"Did you do something?" Naran asked, looking past Tezcatlipoca at the shadowy figure, making him turn to see who Naran was talking to.

"It seems he is from my realm," Quetzal responded, shocking Tezcatlipoca, who fell to the ground and retreated to a corner of the chantli trying to avoid Quetzal.

"Does this mean you didn't help him?"

"Of course not! I thought we were past the trusting issues."

Naran bent down on one knee, looking closely at Tezcatlipoca. *It's remarkable to see him this way.* "You couldn't have found my real name by yourself. Tell me, who helped you?"

"I… is he going to hurt me?"

Naran turns to look at Quetzal and motions him to disappear. *If he is this scared to see one of his kind, he is not aware of what he is.* "Now, can you answer my question?"

"The princess, she said that you were a servant of the gods and were given special gifts. Then you were exiled from the sacred land. I didn't believe her until that day."

Then, why does he look like a human? Could it be because he is one of them? But why did he change till now? "What else did the princess tell you?"

Regaining his courage, Tezcatlipoca stood up, facing Naran. "She told me that when I agreed with her, the gods would erase my sins."

"Quetzal," Naran said, making the shadowy figure appear again, and this time, Tezcatlipoca stood in place. "How can this be?"

"Maybe he awakens his unconsciousness without letting him know."

"Explain"

"Humans' brains have two parts: the unconscious and the conscious, usually the second one is not aware of the first one."

"But he is not human."

"He must have possessed a human and stayed inside for too long, making them one."

"Why didn't that happen to us?"

Quetzal stood quiet. *Maybe he doesn't know either.*

"What is that thing?" said Tezcatlipoca, interrupting Naran and Quetzal's conversation.

Ever since Naran met Tezcatlipoca, he had wished for an opportunity to shock his world. Make him feel as guilty as Naran felt when he found out the truth about the supposed gods. Now he had his chance. With a mischievous smile, he answered, "a god."

Tezcatlipoca's face turned pale "that... can't be," he said with difficulty.

"This is the god that you want so desperately to please."

"Naran," said Quetzal interfering with his dark desires

"What!"

"If you keep this up, you will damage his brain. At this point, he is more human than a god."

"In the end, he is one of yours."

Naran turns to Tezcatlipoca, ready to unleash everything, when Quetzal steps in between them, "you don't have time for this."

"Why do you stop me now? Why didn't you stop me when I killed all of those children?" It was the first time Naran mentioned the tragic event. Yet, Quetzal stood quiet and did not move, which only exasperated Naran. It was also the first time Quetzal confronted him. The first time he had intervened selfishly, making Naran wonder if, at this point, Quetzal was worthier than him. After all, the only sin he had committed was killing a lot fewer people than him. Naran retreated to his chair. Meanwhile, Tezcatlipoca stood there silently with a confused look on his face, unsure of what to make of this.

"I will leave Tula," Naran said, making Tezcatlipoca remember why he was there in the first place.

"When?"

"Soon, now leave." He knew it was too risky to stand up and force Naran to depart this instant, so without saying anything else, Tezcatlipoca left the chantli.

"Did you help him because he is one of yours?" Naran said without breaking eye contact with Quetzal

"I don't care about anyone else, just you."

The laughter that erupted from Naran's lips made him remember that it has been a long time since he laughed or felt anything other than guilt. "Oh Quetzal, in this life, I don't like you," he said with a bright smile. *I am starting to act like him,* he thought with resentment.

"I don't need you to like me. I need you to survive."

The smile turns into a thin line. *Surviving is a waste of time.*

"Why? Wouldn't it be better to end my misery?"

"Dying won't give you peace."

"Why are you so sure?"

"Because I know you."

The response annoyed Naran more than he expected, "Not this again. I thought we agreed on the fact that I am not her and don't want to be, ever."

"You care too much for these people to just selfishly die and leave them to Kinich Ahau."

What bothered him more of that sentence was the confidence with which Quetzal had said it. "Weren't you there when I killed all of those innocent children?"

"You didn't know what they were."

I used that excuse too, thought Naran, "yet you did. You tried to stop me once and then decided to stay silent."

"I didn't stay silent. You blocked me. I was unable to stop you."

"Oh, so now you are the good one, and I am the bad one?"

"At this point, that doesn't matter. Just know this, if you don't stop Kinich Ahau, you will regret it for the rest of your life."

"Humans don't live that long, and I could always kill myself."

It was the first time Naran heard Quetzal sigh as if he had given up and needed to say what he was holding in secret "you are not going to be human for much longer."

"What?"

"I am disappearing, and you are becoming more powerful. What does that tell you?" Naran immediately stood up, "and your conscious is in sync with your unconscious," Quetzal continued

"How long have you known?" said Naran with concern

"For a while. I tried to stop it, but it's useless. Maybe when I disappear completely, you will be able to control the way you see the humans."

Pacing back and forth, not sure what to make of this, Naran asked, "so would I be like Tezcatlipoca?"

"No, I think Kinich Ahau only awakened a part of his unconscious, enough for him to become his true self in appearance. He kept his human ways."

"By human ways, you mean?"

"He doesn't know who he really is or was, yet his body remembers. We, on the other hand, have coexisted together."

Chapter 15

He never liked Quetzal, never understood him, never really cared what he had gone through. Now that there is a possibility of him disappearing, a certain feeling of sadness started to show in Naran's heart. Despite all, he was a companion—someone who had gone through similar things. He had seen the worst of him. As much as Naran wanted to pretend, Quetzal is his only friend. On the other hand, if Quetzal was gone, he would be powerful enough to defeat Kinich Ahau.

"I'm only afraid of one thing." Naran looked at Quetzal, for a moment forgetting he was there. "The guilt, the sadness, and how empty you feel gives you a tendency to act wrongly towards others."

"I was just playing with him, Quetzal," Naran said, smiling as he recalled Tezcatlipoca's scared face.

"If you act like this with the little power you have now, as soon as I'm gone, the darkness will end up consuming you." All amusement left Naran's face. He had also noticed the lack of empathy and compassion he felt for others. *I'm turning like him,* he thought with self-loathing as he remembered the touch of Kinich Ahau.

Dismissing the thought and focusing on the present, Naran realized it was too risky to wait and see what would happen once Quetzal disappeared. "Is there a way you can possess someone else?"

"I'm too weak for that."

"And if I die?"

"I would end up dying too."

Naran kept pacing back and forth, thinking of a way to keep a portion of Quetzal essence from disappearing altogether. "And if I give you back some of the power you lent me?"

Small laughter came from the shadowy figure, making Naran smile a bit. "I don't even know how you were able to consume me in the first place" he looked at Naran with empathetic eyes. "Are you now scared of losing me?"

"I'm scared of who I will become once you are gone." They both went silent again because they shared the same fear.

Within a few days, Naran's world had changed completely. He had left the only thing he had known his entire life. For better or for worse, he had to deal with the consequences of his actions. Even if, in truth, Kinich Ahau hadn't given him much of a choice. Nonetheless, he had to finish what he had started one way or another.

Morning arrived, and with a fresh mind, Naran asked Quetzal to sit. He had been thinking of all sorts of ideas, and he needed to run them by Quetzal. "Kinich Ahau said several times that you two were like one. Is there a way you can bend light like he did? If the problem is my conscience, maybe we can delete it or hide it."

Quetzal looked up and let out a sigh, then faced Naran. "He didn't bend light. Certain objects were made for us. Most of them have been destroyed, although it seems he kept a few."

With that being said, Naran tried another route "What if we forget who we are?"

"Again, that can only be done with the object Kinich Ahau has. Besides, it would be impossible to hide things from one another."

"Then how was it possible that Tezcatiploca forgot who he is?"

"My guess is that he possessed a human trying to hide from our kind, and at some point, he started to become one with the person. This must-have altered both their knowledge."

"I don't understand."

"Kinich Ahau told us that if we wanted to hide from our elders, we could always possess a human," Quetzal stopped. His eyes widened a bit, almost as if he realized something. "Now that I think about it, maybe he said that to trick us. He specifically avoided mentioning the fact that if we stay too long in a body, we would forget who we are and become human."

If this is true, maybe if we remind all those gods who they really are, and tell them that it was Kinich Ahau's fault, then together we might have a chance to defeat him. "Then why don't we help them remember, and they might regain their abilities."

"The human brain is too fragile. I explained that already." And with that, all Naran's hopes died. They were back to square one, although the more he questioned, the less ignorant he felt. Most of the time, he had to play along. Now he had someone who could answer his 'whys,' this was the perfect opportunity to finally learn about their kind and history. "How did you end up stuck with Kinich Ahau?"

Quetzal's eyes widened as he took in the question Naran asked, "he binds us together." His voice had a hint of nostalgia, and Naran couldn't help but feel sad for the life Quetzal had to endure. Up until now, he had been a mere shadow with eyes. Yet, he was once like Kinich Ahau. "I was sentenced to death for interacting and killing humans. Kinich Ahau came and rescued me. I was moved by his actions. So, I thought he meant no harm. He was a brother to me," he paused for a second and smiled weakly. "Then he tried to convince me that humans were not worth it, that because of them, I almost died. At first, I did believe him, and then I met her. He seemed to be fine with me doing this, so we made a deal. However, he broke his promise, and we fought. I was able to conceal part of his energy, but it weakened me, allowing him to reduce me to this shadow. He threatened me by holding your... her life."

Shocked by the mention of the word brother and the thought of Quetzal having a family, Naran asked, "Does this mean you have parents?"

The corner of Quetzal's eyes shrunk upwards, which made Naran think that maybe he was smiling. "When I said he was like a brother to me, I meant that all of my kind are like a family. We are born differently." He took a moment, then continued, "I would say it's similar to the miaccîtlalli. You don't know where or when, yet suddenly there is a new xitlalli. That's why I say we are all connected." The expression of confusion on Naran's face made Quetzal elaborate a bit more. "If it helps you, think of us like an evolution of humankind. The biggest difference —I would say— we have is that we were born without malice. Our purpose and core are to learn about everything and anything. Expand our energy or powers, whichever you like. The problem is that learning comes hand in hand with curiosity. So, when your kind appears, showing all those emotions... Well, you already know the rest. That's when Kinich Ahau turned into who it is now," said Quetzal. The way the shadowy figure moved suggested he had been in a tense posture until now he seemed to be relaxing.

All of this made partial sense to Naran. He wondered if they had no idea what emotions are, how is it that every time he speaks of her or talks about his past, it sounds like he is feeling love and sadness.

Naran placed both feet flat on the ground, getting ready to talk about a subject that, even to him, was a mystery. "So, your kind is not capable of loving?"

"It's not that we don't love. It's that we do it differently." Quetzal looked up for a few minutes as if he was thinking hard on something "for example, you see a tree and feel nothing because it's wood and leaves to you. We see the light of different colors passing through each branch and leaf. Then we try to understand its purpose, and when we do, we begin to love it. We don't take ownership of that tree, we don't need that tree for personal reasons, we let it be, and that makes us happy."

It all seemed to Naran like a big charade because if what Quetzal said was true, then why would all this chaos happen? "Are admiring things boring to you?" burst Naran without thinking.

It took a moment for Quetzal to answer, "why would we be bored? There are millions of things to discover, to understand, and love."

This still did not clarify Naran's question. "The fact that so many of you ended up among us means that you weren't content in your little world," he said again without thinking.

"Loving something freely by understanding its truth makes us content and happy. However, happiness it's not our goal in life. Our goal it's to learn, and when we do, we get to experience happiness, and we don't make decisions based on that, nor is it our motivation. The reason many of us fell into your realm was the need to fulfill our curiosity, to learn and understand why it is that you do things the way you do."

"So much for a superior race."

Quetzal chuckled at Naran's comment, "Yes, it seems we also made mistakes."

"Does this mean that you acquired our customs?"

"I don't understand." It was the first time Naran felt a bit superior to Quetzal.

"You keep using the names humans gave you. Kinich Ahau refers to you as Quetzalcoatl and vice versa."

"Ah yes, well, maybe you are right. It is easier that way. However, we don't own a name. That's a necessity to your kind: to name everything. For us, it is more important to know how things work than what we should call it."

They stayed quiet while Naran's brain was trying to grasp all the information given, and Quetzal waited patiently to answer all of his questions.

After a few minutes of digesting their conversation, Naran asked. "Earlier, you said that the only way you could hide from one another was by entering this realm and possessing humans. What did you mean by that?"

He took a deep breath before answering, "since we all have the same goal, there is no need to lie or to be in each other's business. We simply carry on. However, we had one rule: do not disturb or interfere with any life, including your kind. So, when we had a taste of your emotions, we broke the only rule we had. It became impossible to stop or let go; hence the need to hide."

"Does this mean you knew there were more of your kind here?"

"Many of us broke the rule during the 'falling in love' incident. The higher and most powerful of all of us got rid of all the lawbreakers. That's when Kinich Ahau saved me and condemned me. I thought nobody else had survived, but it seems I was wrong." Quetzal looked to the side. "What alarms me the most is that I wasn't able to identify Tezcatlipoca until now."

"You said that you can hide from one another by being inside of a human, so how did that god find you?"

"Nobody can hide from him, and the fact that one survived makes me wonder if it was someone else's doing."

"When you say 'from him,' you mean the Ometeotl?" said Naran. As a reflex, the eyes of Quetzal shrank again, which by now Naran inferred as a smile.

"If it helps you understand it by naming it, yes, we can call it Ometeotl."

With this, Naran understood the explanation Quetzal gave. Yet, the need to name things was more than just a fancy. It was a way to communicate between the different altepetl and have understandable words for everything. Although it made sense that this comment made Quetzal smile. As they locked eyes, there was one thing Naran was eager to know. "Why her? Don't you have any females of your kind?"

Automatically at the mention of her, the eyes of Quetzal showed sorrow and sadness. It amazed Naran how a pair of eyes could express this much emotion. "She was the first one to approach me when I felt all these emotions. It only took her warm smile for me to give up everything. For the first time, I wanted something that only I could have." His voice became affectionate, making Naran's heart feel less heavy.

"It could have been anyone, not necessarily her."

"Yes"

"What if she didn't want you in the same way?"

Quetzal stood silent, narrowing his eyes at Naran as if suggesting something. Then it hit Naran.

"Ah, right, right, I apologize."

He had been talking and asking questions as if he was a bystander when he was the cause for all this commotion. It was clear to Naran that they were the root of all this mess. It did not matter how many of them entered the human realm. Quetzalcoatl, Kinich Ahau, and he had destroyed entire civilizations, had killed innocent people, had altered the environment, and had made it out alive without a scratch.

There were other things that Naran wanted to discuss with Quetzal, for instance, their Ometeotl. However, time was running out for Quetzal, and they needed to find a solution quickly.

"There are three altepetl left: the Zapotec, Mixtec, and Mayan. It will take us four and a half days to get to the Zapotec altepetl. From what I have been gathering, the Mixtec altepetl has settlements along the route we will take. The closest is a day and a half from here. Our best option is to try and gather as much information as possible. There are records of your kind, I'm sure of it. We just need to find their location." Naran said this with such determination that it made him feel alive again. Maybe all he needed was a purpose that provided some sort of hope.

Chapter 16

The moment he walked out of Tula, Naran experienced mixed emotions. The fear of the uncertain, anguish for the lives that would be lost if he failed, and doubts about not being strong enough to defeat a god. At the same time, these feelings made him smile. It had been a long time since he felt like himself, like a human. Having such marvelous abilities that gave him strength and courage made him forget his true self; forget why he was indecisive and fearful. *It feels as if I have been pretending this whole time*. He dismissed the thought quickly and tried to focus on the road.

The sun began to fall, and Naran wondered how things would be now that Tezcatlipoca was in charge. Without a doubt, he would bring back the sacrifices. Naran hoped that after everything he did, people would question Tezcatlipoca's actions. Become skeptical about how killing someone was the right way —or the only way— to satisfy the gods.

His lack of knowledge about traveling surprised Naran. There were moments that he reached a dead road and had to turn back to start all over again. With no people around to ask and having decided to avoid summoning Quetzal to save up his energy —unless there was an emergency, he had to figure it out by himself.

Before leaving, he received instructions of what path to take from a local traveler in Tula. He thought it would be easy, but now that he was actually walking, the roads seem to merge and create new ones or divide in two, sometimes three. Thankfully he had the river that helped him situate himself. For the first time, most of his abilities were useless. The only ones that benefited him were being able to survive without water or food.

"Do you give up?" the shadowy figure appeared beside Naran, making him stop

"We agreed that you would stay inside."

"I doubt it makes any difference."

Naran signed and agreed with Quetzal. "I have probably made a wrong turn somewhere."

"Try and climb that mountain over there." Naran followed Quetzal's finger and did as told. He had no mental strength to argue anymore. Reaching the top, he saw in the distance a complex teôcalli. *They seem more evolved than the other altepetl I have witnessed,* Naran thought as he sat down to admire the sunset.

"Is that the place?"

"Probably. I have never traveled this far before." They stood silent, watching how the sky turned dark and small lights appeared in the distance. *There has to be someone in that altepetl that could aid us.* Naran looked at Quetzal, wanting to ask more about his kind, yet he decided to keep silent. If curiosity had brought them to this deplorable state, it would be best if he continued to ignore his personal questions.

Time felt heavy with each step Naran took. Losing against Kinich Ahau was no longer a problem. What bothered him now was who he would become. He was pleased by thinking he was a good person, someone who did what he was told, who had bothered no one, and kept to himself. Until, of course, the moment he took away his mother's life. Thus, when Kinich Ahau appeared asking for Naran's help, he felt he had a chance to prove his worthiness by helping a god and obeying. However, deep down, he was actually looking for a way to cleanse his past.

They arrived in the morning, taking longer than what Naran had initially planned. He changed his clothing into what he could only assume was appropriate —as he remembered when he was still able to see people as humans. When he entered the altepetl and encountered all the deteriorated creatures, his heart began to pound, and his vision turned blurry. *If we don't fix this soon, it will end up causing me trouble,* he thought, taking a deep breath, hoping that they didn't stand out of the crowd.

Naran tried to avoid eye contact. "Excuse me, do you know where his greatness resides?" He asks, avoiding any word that could risk alerting the person that they were outsiders. Given that he wasn't sure they used the same term used for nobility.

"At the west side of the teôcalli." *That was simple enough.* He thought as he walked, trying to avoid any contact with anyone.

When he arrived, warriors blocked his path as he tried to reach the chantli. "Commoners are not welcome past this point."

Same class prejudice thought Naran, remembering how it was to be born in the low ranks. "I have information from Tula regarding Ce Acatl Quetzalcoatl." The servicemen looked at each other, not sure of what to do.

"Let him in," said a rough voice from inside. *Their chantli is much more elaborate.* Naran thought, admiring the structure as he walked inside. "Well, what is it?" said an old man with a harsh voice, sitting in an icpalli similar to the one Kinich Ahau had. With a glance, Naran notices the cozcatl made of a smooth black texcalli and on his lap a much wider one. This indicated he was in the presence of a Teopixqui.

"I have been sent on behalf of the gods," said Naran turning the tables, making the old man tense in his seat.

Clearing his throat while his companions murmured among themselves, "You insolent fool, how dare you speak to me that way!"

Naran smiled, thinking how easily he could kill the old man. However, the thought took away his smile. *I'm not going to do that anymore.* "I think it would be best if we speak alone." Naran's voice was confident and firm that the old man, without thinking, dismissed his company. Naran got rid of his disguise showing his true self —the one Kinich Ahau created.

Such a display made the old man hold his breath, "w-who are you?"

"That is not important. I'm sorry to deceive you, but I have an urgent problem that I need to solve. Quetzal, show yourself." And without warning, Quetzal appeared frightening the poor man nearly to death. He then immediately fell to his knees and bowed. "Your excellency. To what do I owe the great honor of having you in the presence of this lowly-born servant of yours?" Said the man with a shaky voice. *Even he knew his inferiority.*

"Stand up. I hate it when humans bow. It makes me feel responsible for their wellbeing."

Chapter 17

Naran never ventured on the reasons behind the order of eradication. It never occurred to him the importance that the altepetl had with one another. Mainly because he was always busy eliminating or ruling. Therefore, he had no time to stop and think deeply of the consequences that would unfold once an altepetl ceased to exist. Within a few days with the Mixtecs, he discovers that each altepetl has specific functionality that forces them to collaborate with one another.

When the Teotihuacan altepetl —the largest and most developed of all, disappeared it created an imbalance. The power shifted. The Olmec altepetl perished soon after, not by Kinich Ahau as Naran thought but by a small group of warriors led by an unknown Teopixqui who Naran could guess was another god trap in a human.

Naran's fear would come true if things kept going as they are; the Toltec altepetl would succumb soon. *Could it be that the plan of Kinich Ahau is to destroy every altepetl? Why didn't he do it himself? Where in this plan do Quetzal and I stand?* That thought made him feel incompetent and the most inadequate person for the task of saving humankind.

He never thought that learning to read or write was necessary knowledge. Thankfully his mother didn't care what he thought and forced him to learn. Because of this, he was able to read the Mixtec records in two days. They talk about different gods and how —based on their knowledge— the world was created. Naran found descriptions of the forms of Quetzal, Kinich Ahau, and others, yet nothing on what he needed to know. However, the mention of how these Mixtec early rulers founded their cities and established their territories gave him insights into why Kinich Ahau started with the Teotihuacan altepetl.

Looking in the maps of the location of each altepetl, Naran realized they took a wrong turn which led them to this particular place. He also found out that the Mixtecs devote their workforce to obtaining the raw obsidian texcalli, more commonly known as iztli. Then later transforming it into weapons and cozcatl, which explains the wardrobe and the strange texcalli they possess.

The natural light that helped read started to die down, which could only mean that the night was approaching, and he kept reading the same scroll, unable to comprehend. Standing up to stretch —which has been a long time since he last did that— Naran could feel the eyes of the Teopixqui, probably wondering if he was safe or not. *Why does he keep touching that iztli circle with such earnestness?* Naran thought as he noticed the hands of the Teopixqui.

"What is the story behind the iztli?"
The heart of the Teopixqui became used to hearing Naran speak without warning at a high volume "When used as a reflection, we cleanse our soul. When used as a weapon, the soul is sent to the

gods."

Naran heard Quetzal chuckle at the given explanation, appearing behind the Teopixqui then heading to the iztli circle that lay next to the scrolls. "It's just a texcalli." The shadowy fingers touch the surface of the supposedly texcalli, and a sudden scream leaves his absent lips. "What on earth is that?!"

The agitation and shock in Quetzal's voice made Naran reach for the artifact and pick it up.

"Did it hurt you when you touched it?"

"that's a stupid question, don't you think!" Quetzal step back, afraid of the iztli

"it's not made for gods," the Teopixqui said casually

"You could have shared that piece of information from the beginning!"

"Forgive me, your grace, I'm still recovering from-"

"I know! Anything else we should know?" The exasperation in Quetzal's voice made it clear that it hurt him deeply. Naran toned out of the conversation and took out his sword. The whole blade all the way to the point had a color similar to the iztli

"Quetzal"

"What?!"

"Grab my sword."

"I will not do that!"

The gaze that Naran gave Quetzal had such intensity that Quetzal couldn't disobey. With his left hand, he grabbed the grip of the sword, waiting for the worst, yet nothing happened.

"Touch the edge of the blade." Quetzal sighs and, with his right hand, reaches for the edge.

As soon as it comes into contact, Quetzal lets another scream, "satisfied!"

Naran grabs the sword from Quetzal's hand and touches the edge of the sword, feeling nothing "interesting."

"I haven't seen an iztli weapon so detailed and elegant as yours." Teopixqui approached Naran and extended his hands, asking for permission to touch the sword. "It's magnificent," he said, savoring the word in his lips. *What does 'send the souls to the gods' mean?* Naran's question made him fear the hidden intentions of Kinich Ahau when he gave him that sword. "What else can't the gods touch?"

"I only knew that from my ancestors, and I wasn't sure if it was true or a lie until now," he said with an apologetic tone which made Naran believe he was telling the truth.

"Did your ancestors mention anything else?"

After a few minutes of thinking, the Teopixqui said, "a day from here to the southwest, there is another Mixtec altepetl. I heard of a texcalli that has special elements."

"That could be any stone-"

"Sshhh," Naran shushes Quetzal so that he could think what to do next "is there someone that could guide us there?"

"Certainly! I would send my trusted man to accompany you." the Teopixqui left for a moment to speak with a small boy, leaving the iztli circle unattended.

Quetzal took that moment to whisper to Naran, "it will be better if we travel alone. He could-"

"I can't risk getting lost again" the determination that shows in Naran's eyes made it clear that nothing was going to stop him.

Teopixqui came back inside just in time to hear Naran said "we leave before sunrise" he then left, making Quetzal disappear in the process. "If you can't touch this sword, there must be other things that affect you," Naran said rather loudly, making a few people turn "he mentioned cleansing the soul. I think I know how to do it."

He then turns right and heads to a lake nearby.

Chapter 18

Somewhere along the way, Naran's heart shifted positions. He tried to conceal the struggle but seeing the number of creatures clouded his judgment ever since entering this altepetl. Even though Quetzal is still intact, Naran keeps feeling the urge to kill everyone, fully aware they are humans. Hence the urgency to regain his sight back at all cost. There is a chance that after this, nothing changes, and he would have to face the consequences, at least he tried. Naran's feet reached the water, took out the iztli circle —that turns out to be a mirror— of the Teopixqui. *If I don't fix this, I fear the darkness will end up consuming me sooner than expected,* he thought as his fingers pressed down its surface. "A long time ago, when I was wandering near a river, I saw a man with strange clothing holding a black texcalli. He was speaking in a different dialect, and when he finished, something from his body left and entered the texcalli. I was mesmerized by what I saw."

"You want to put me inside the mirror?"

"No, I don't think that's possible. What I want is to gain my sight back".

Unable to recall the exact words, Naran tried several times to emulate the movements of that fuzzy memory just to fail every time.

"You are doing it wrong," said a female voice. *Could it be a Kinich Ahau disguise again?* he thought, avoiding looking, dreading to find a creature "you need to sanctify it first. With your finger, draw three circles to the right, and while you draw them, breathe deeply ten times."

Naran kept looking at the mirror, not moving or turning. *I have nothing to lose* with that thought in mind. He closed his eyes and did as instructed, then turned to where he heard the female voice without opening his eyes. "What else?"

"That depends on what you want to achieve?"

"I don't understand."

"You don't look like a Teopixqui, which means that you are not trying to give your soul willingly. Makes me wonder how you got that mirror."

Naran sighs, feeling impatient. "I have a problem with my eyes," he said, ignoring the girl's inquisition.

"Ah! Well, then, submerge the mirror in the water, carefully drink from its surface what it gathers, then open your eyes and see your reflection, focus on your eyes. Soon you will see your face disappearing completely. When that happens, clear your mind and breath ten times, but do not close your eyes."

As he began doing what the girl said, the image that reflected in the mirror kept making him lose his focus. *Just focus on the eyes.* He thought, trying to build courage. After a few seconds, his face was gone leaving Naran perplexed. *How is this possible?*

"Remember to breathe," said the female voice, making Naran

concentrate.

Naran's mind kept rambling on thoughts such as why their appearance changed, but the voice sounded human, and he could identify if it was a female or a male voice. Even if they were deformed, they usually have something that makes them look human, either an eye, arm, leg, fingers or even belly bottoms. *You are distracting yourself Naran,* it has been a long time since he heard Quetzal's voice inside his head, and it was enough for him to finish the ritual. He closes his eyes and breath one last time.

"Don't be afraid," she said, and Naran couldn't help the smile *between the two of us. You should be the one afraid,* yet the thought only made him worry because if it turns out it didn't work and he keeps seeing monsters instead of humans, it might be the end for him.

He opened his eyes, turned towards the girl, and found a young woman with long black hair, brown eyes, and rosy heart-shaped lips. Her skin tone revealed she was no slave nor common collector but of a higher-class lady. The sight captivates him until the fear appears. "Is she human?"

Quetzal emerges next to Naran, making the poor girl fall. "It seems she is." With his confirmation, Naran falls to his knees and cries, letting out all his frustration. The scene could make anyone feel sympathy for him, and Quetzal was no exception, his shadowy hand resting on Naran's shoulder trying to comfort him.

He had been struggling with dark thoughts, fighting a battle between what he knew and what he saw. In this moment and despite what he made himself believe, the events of when her mother died unfold before him. Her mother lay in the middle of the chakmoli, both of them surrounded by people who shout and scream blood. His shaky hands could barely hold the tecpatl given to him, the feeling of helplessness when they ordered him to choose between his life and his mother's. The moment he locked eyes with his mother, he couldn't do it. And as the last act of love, with a sweet smile and eyes full of compassion, his mother took his hand and perforated her heart. It was the first time he recalled the actual events, but it didn't make it easier. It didn't take away his guilt. If anything, it made him feel worse. Since that tragic day, he altered the facts of what happened and made sure no one, not even Quetzal, found out the truth.

"Who are you?" said the girl bringing Naran back to the present, remembering they were not alone.

"Is there a way to make her forget?" said Naran after clearing his throat. Even after gaining his sight back, it didn't liberate him from becoming a revolting human being, and Quetzal was aware of this. "I don't think it's a good idea to do that."

"I-I promise I won't tell," said the girl with a shaky voice that revealed how scared she was. As for Naran, for a brief moment, the thought of killing her crossed his mind.

"Very well go now," said Quetzal urging the girl while holding Naran in place. She ran as fast as she could, and when she became out of sight, Quetzal let go. "That was not necessary. I wasn't going to hurt her."

"I can hear your every thought, and it bothers me that even when you saw her as a normal human, you still favored to harmed her"

"I can't help thinking about such stuff, but it doesn't mean I'm going to act on it!" Naran stood up, cleaning his clothes and stepping out of the lake. "It's fine if you don't trust me. At this point, I don't even trust myself. However, I don't think you fully understand what I have to deal with. You know what you are and who you are. You know your limitations. As for me... Quetzal, I don't even feel like a human anymore. Even when I was a human, I didn't have courage or compassion or anything! Kinich Ahau gave me all that, for better or for worse" Naran sat down, resting his back on the trunk of the tree, feeling a bit defeated. "I had nothing, and I was nothing. Therefore, I understand why the moment I get more power, I will get corrupted. Didn't you see I was already rotten before any of you showed up? The difference is back then, the only one I would have harmed was myself."

Quetzal approach Naran and try to console him again "Naran they made you kill your mother it wasn't-"

"They gave me a choice!"

"And you choose to survive."

Naran laughed at Quetzal's comment, "you have been far too long in this realm. If the old you, before the humans, saw all this, what would he have said?"

Quetzal sighs, "a life is a life, doesn't matter what it does, no one should take it."

"And how would you fix this?"

"I wasn't made to fix or to modify. I could simply observe and preserve"

"So, what are you doing here?"

Quetzal's eyes widened because he had also asked himself this question "I'm preserving a life that I hold dear."

"Well, I don't want you to do that. I want you to let me go."

"I... can't."

"can't or don't want to."

"What difference does it make, Naran?! At this point, who cares if I stay or go, I already did enough damage to your realm, and if I can do something to fix just a portion of it, then I would do it."

The sun hides behind the mountains letting the light of xitlalli cover the sky "how are you going to fix something when you don't even know what 'fix' means. And that's just, to begin with because I'm not sure you understand what being human actually is. It's not only to breathe or eat or drink. It's far more complex than that. I'm sure you have never experienced two sets of emotions that contradict themselves. Heck, I don't even think you have experienced loneliness to its fullest. The only thing you experience is love and the short period of happiness that provides."

"I watch her die, so don't go around assuming-"

"Oh, poor Quetzal, you watch someone you love die. I have killed someone I love. I have watched people dear to me die constantly. Death is part of our realm, whether you know the person or not. Thousands of innocent people die as an offer to your kind because you couldn't stop your stupid curiosity. You have no right to feel guilty or sad for any of us!"

The shadowy figure lay down on the ground, making it hard for Naran to distinguish his edges "you're right. What do you want me to do?"

This time Naran sigh, feeling his anger slowly melted down. "You couldn't even get my sight back. I had to find a way for myself" the sounds of the insects made the silence on Naran's head feel less heavy. "You want to know what I wanted a few days ago, Quetzal? I wanted my kind to have a chance without your kind meddling. The more time that passes, the less I care for this"

"What do you think would happen when you gain the rest of my power?"

Naran chuckles and sighs, looking at the sky "indifferent."

"What do you mean by that?"

"You said humans have the tendency for malice, but that depends on who is judging. If the higher authorities tell you to kill someone to save or protect everyone else, you will do it, not out of malice but out of the greater good. After some time, you stop caring for the lost lives and do it out of habit because who would question whether we are doing good or bad. With this in mind, if I gain that power, it would only intensify the feeling of not caring because death is part of my life."

It was the second time Naran explained something to Quetzal. Ever since they met, it has been the other way around. Naran had to keep quiet and pretend he understood what was going on. In reality, he couldn't even comprehend how the light can be bent and manipulated in such a way.

Tired and drained to use his voice, he said one last thing: *You indeed have higher intelligence than any human. That's probably the reason why you are unable to comprehend emotions, thoughts, and feelings. There are far more things than love and loss,* fully knowing that Quetzal could hear his thoughts —most of them anyway.

Chapter 19

The cold wind and unheated sun forecast the beginning of winter. For Naran, this was the worst season of the year. Around this time, the low class would suffer the majority of the damage. Not many would survive. However, this was common. Nobody concerned themselves with the number of deaths. They simply acquired more slaves to compensate.

Taking a moment to see his hands. He remembered when his fingers turned blue, and he quickly started a campfire, praying he didn't lose any of his precious fingers. That's when he realized how crucial his hands were. They were his work tool, and without it, he would become the next in line to be sacrificed or, worse, a slave. With the memory in mind, he notices how the cold breeze doesn't affect him. While the young man that the Teopixqui gave them keeps shivering now and then, evoking in Naran a certain nostalgia. *This might be how Quetzal feels. Knowing you have to feel something yet not experience any sensation*, Naran thought as he eyed the boy with envy.

"Xoaltentli," said Naran taking his cape off and offering it to the boy

"Sir, I-I'm not worthy."

"Neither am I, just take it."

And with that, Xoaltentli took the cape and smiled when he felt the soft fabric with his fingertips. When the cloak was around his shoulder, his eyes widened. Naran took as a sign that Xoaltentli was a simple slave whose life depended on the Teopixqui. In many ways, they were alike.

For some reason, this made Naran curious about if any low class would have done what he did just to feel a bit of importance. "If you were given a chance to be something else, would you take it?" said Naran wanting to feel better for his choices.

"I don't seem to understand, sir."

"If you could be a Tecuhtli or a Teopixqui, would you, do it?"

It took Xoaltentli a moment to grasp what Naran said. He then looked to the ground and said, "I wouldn't dare to be anything else."

"Why?"

"Because that's not who I am, and I don't know how to be anything else."

"What if someone teaches you how to do it?"

Xoaltentli gave Naran a warm smile, almost implying that Naran didn't know how the world work "There are things that shouldn't be taught but be born in"

"I don't understand."

"Look at the birds," says Xoaltentli pointing at the sky. "They are born to fly, and the way they do it is beautiful, but if you get a hen and teach it to fly high like those birds, it would seem wrong to see it moving in the sky."

The words that Xoaltentli uses and his vocabulary are too wise for a slave "What is your position?"

"Sir?"

"What is it that you do?"

"I'm an apprentice."

"Of what?"

"Everything"

"That is a vague answer."

Xoaltentli gave a simple smile to Naran and kept walking. *Who is this person exactly?* The thought stays inside Naran's head. Disappointed by the answer, he rectifies himself. Thinking they were alike was a desperate excuse to try calming the remains of his conscience, trying to find a small hope to save his soul.

Traveling in silence, noticing the leafless trees submerged in thoughts of living and death, Naran walks behind the small slave boy. Sometimes Xoaltentli would suggest stopping to eat or rest, and Naran would simply comply. Even if he no longer needed food nor needed to sleep, he still had to pretend to be human. With no particular purpose, Naran kept brushing with his feet the leaves to the side of the road giving a more straightforward path. Although, there were some parts where there were no leaves, suggesting that many people had walked the same narrow path with an unknown goal. This widened the curiosity that Naran has been neglecting for a while since Quetzal entered his body. Made him wonder about many things that never occurred to him before. For example, why would someone have to travel such a great distance to arrive at a deserted place, transform it and then leave again? *A vicious cycle we have,* he thought while picking a small texcalli from the ground. This thought led him to think about why Kinich Ahau was doing all of this. If he was already a god and a powerful being, what is he trying to achieve? Why did it take him this long if he could have tried it in other lifetimes —if reincarnation is real anyway— Why is this life so unique?

The next day after Xoaltentli woke up, they continued walking until the path became flat and smooth. The mountains that Naran saw yesterday as a tiny point were now getting bigger and bigger.

Mesmerized by the tall mountain, Naran reduced the pace and kept admiring how the clouds hid the top of the hill. Then how the small visible portion under the clouds was covered by white color. "it's the Popocatepetl and his love Iztaccihuatl" Xoaltentli's voice brought Naran back to the present.

Not sure what he was talking about. "Who are they?" he asks.

"Those big mountains, sir. We will be arriving soon."

It seems Quetzal was right about having to name everything he thought. Still, curiosity got the best of him. "What do you mean by his love? It's two simple mountains."

"They were human once."

Naran chuckled, yet seeing how serious Xoaltentli was, he cleared his throat "how did they become that?" said Naran pointing at the mountains

"There are different stories; each altepetl has a version. The most popular one says that war occurred, and Popocatepetl had to leave and fight for his people. Before leaving, he promised to come back and marry Iztaccihuatl. Then after days and nights, a malicious person deceived Iztaccihuatl by saying that

Popocatepetl had perished in the war. Her heart couldn't handle such news, and she died. When the war was over, and Popocatepetl came back victorious, he was told the terrible news. After that day, people saw him wandering around the village, not eating or sleeping. Until one day, he ordered some people to construct a teôcalli where the sun touches the earth. He also told them to build a tumb and place it on the top. Once it was finished, he took the lifeless body of his beloved and placed it there, giving her one last kiss. He stayed there with a torch keeping his promise of staying by her side. Since that day, they have never been separated."

Why do people do such foolish things for love? I don't understand what drives them to the point of no return? The thought created a pressure in his chest that he never felt before, and he could only imagine the reason behind it. Dismissing it quickly, he asks, "alright, and how did they end up becoming a mountain?"

"The gods felt sorry for them and transformed them to keep them together."

Why would a god do that? The gods I know would definitely not. "I don't think they have such power."

"Tales are tales sir. They might hide the truth even if it's a small one."

Recalling his conversations with the last Tecuhtli made Naran wonder if Xoaltentli might have something to add. "Is there any tale about a special texcalli that does things to a god?"

After a moment of thinking, he responded, "There was an old tale that said that a variety of objects were made by sacrifices of powerful Teopixqui. Each of them had enormous powers that could make anyone a god. However, if this is true, it wouldn't be easy to found" It could be possible that these things exist, but Naran didn't want to become a god. He needed to conceal a real one.

They arrive at the entrance of the altepetl. Everyone seemed to be oblivious to the things that had happened. Nobody seemed to be worried about the devastation that had been happening. Xoaltentli kept his promise of delivering them safe and sound, then he left as quietly as he arrived. Naran went directly to the Teopixqui of the altepetl, not caring about the restrictions of class rank. Something warned him that time was running out.

Days fly by, and no matter how hard Naran tries to get people to talk about the 'texcalli,' they just look at each other and dismiss him quickly. The last option was to speak with the Tecuhtli, but he left for the Zapotec altepetl, and no one knows when exactly he is coming back. *Why is it that every time I take a step forward, I am pushed two steps back?* Naran thought, hoping that Quetzal would answer, but he had gone quiet, and Naran feared the worst. He sat on a vast texcalli at the base of the Popocatepetl defeated

"Sir?" Naran turned to see Xoaltentli's smiling face. "I thought it was you. Is everything alright?"

Naran sighs, not sure if it would make any difference. "No, I can't find this special 'texcalli."

"Why do you need that?"

"I'm not sure if I need it or not. I just know that it might be an answer." Xoaltentli handed back the cape to Naran and sat on the floor. "I gave this to you. I don't need it."

"It will go to waste if I keep it." Naran put the cape on. It was pointless to think he would feel any warmth. "What is that question that you are desperately trying to find an answer to?"

"It's complicated."

"Try me, sir."

Naran sight again "If you could... kill a god. How would you do it?"

"it's impossible" Xoaltentli's answer made Naran chuckle because he was aware of that. He waited for Naran to compose himself then continued, "if not even a human can't die, what makes you believe a god can? Sir, the human flesh is just a vessel that holds the essence, the vessel has an expiration date, but the essence is infinite. If you ask me, the only difference between a god and us is that vessel."

Making him speechless and unable to react to the unexpected piece of information. It took a moment for Naran to grasp what Xoaltentli said. "If what you're saying is true, then humans would have extraordinary abilities."

"And who says they don't have them, sir? A woman and man can create life if they work together. They can endure hardships every day-"

"Those are not extraordinary abilities," said Naran, cutting off Xoaltentli, who smiled, unbothered by the interruption.

"Sir, sometimes reality eats fantasy." With that, he got up and walked to the edge of a cliff. "Don't trouble yourself with those thoughts, sir. Sometimes ignorance is a blessing" he looked at Naran, giving him one last smile, then took a step back and fell down the cliff.

Naran woke up sweating and unable to recall how or when exactly he fell asleep. He tried desperately to clear his mind, unsure if it was a dream or an actual event, "Quetzalcoatl!" Naran said at the top of his lungs.

The shadowy figure appeared more quickly than usual "what happened?"

Naran couldn't find his words. His brain was a considerable node "I-I... he, he just fell, I saw him, and-"

"Naran, you are not making any sense. Why don't you try to sleep more?"

"No, no, we need to find the texcalli and, and-"

"The Tecuhtli hasn't arrived yet. We would have to wait"
He didn't need sleep yet for some reason. A heavy feeling in his eyes and body begged him to rest. Unsure and a bit nervous, he went back to sleep.

Dreamless and well-rested, Naran walked to the teôcalli gardens, where the Tecuhtli was waiting for him. This was the last opportunity he had to figure out where he could find the texcalli or if there was such a thing. Upon arriving, he noticed how young the Tecuhtli looked. He was standing very calm, then saw Naran approaching and met him halfway. With a bright smile, he introduced himself then asked with a hint of amusement, "Naran. Where are you from?"

"The Olmec altepetl," said Naran avoiding mentioning exact locations.

"You have to travel a great distance to get here."
Ignoring the conversation entirely and desperate for answers,

Naran went right to what he needed to know "How was your trip to the Zapotec altepetl?"

Naran's behavior made the Tecuhtli smile briefly. Nonetheless, he responded calmly, "it was longer than expected." He put his hands behind his back. "I'm not used to speaking with people of your kind. From what I have been told, you escalated by threatening people."

The way he spoke made Naran lose the small amount of patience he had "the texcalli."

"Ah yes, I have also been told you have turned the entire altepetl upside down looking for this texcalli, but I'm afraid there is no such thing in this place."

"You are lying."

"Or someone lied to you."

Although what he said was a possibility, Naran was not in the mood to play mind games. "Quetzal, show yourself." Contrary to the reaction of the Mixtec Teopixqui, this Tecuhtli remains calm and serene when the shadowy figure appears next to Naran. "What do you say now?"

The Tecuhtli look from Quetzal to Naran and smile "I don't know anything about texcalli." The shadowy figure grew in size trying to intimidate the old man, yet it made no reaction. "The problem is that your little friend is no longer considered a god" he said as a response to his lack of fear.

"What?"

"He is a mere shadow of what he used to be. I don't serve inferior gods," said Tecuhtli with an air of superiority.

Naran grabbed him by the neck enough to make it hard for the man to breathe correctly "you might not fear him, but you should fear me, now answer me!"

"I-I don't-"

"That's not what I want to hear."

"Naran, stop. You are going to kill him," said Quetzal, urging Naran to remember he had vowed not to hurt any other human.

Against his desires, he loses the grip a bit "try speaking again."

"w-we have iztli and o-other precious-"

Not what he wanted to hear, he decided to let go, making the Tecuhtli fall to the ground, recovering his breath. After a few minutes, Naran decided to try another route. "Alright, tell me a way to conceal this shadow so that it doesn't disappear."

The Tecuhtli get up, clean himself and face Naran. "If such a thing is possible, it could only be found in the Mayan territory. There is a teôcalli named Chichen Itza." He said calmly, "I sent a group of warriors to gather some cozcatl." The thought that someone would ignore the current state of devastation and death just to gather a few cozcatl made Naran chuckle and feel less bad about himself. "My men were too afraid to touch that place."

Even if this was true, Naran doesn't have the time required to travel such a distance. "How can you be so certain that the Chichen Itza could help me conceal the shadow?"

"My Teopixqui, he had a revelation where a god trembled in fear as he was trapped in that place."

Naran grabs the Tecuhtli by the collar "it seems that you are wasting my time."

"I-I swear to you this is-"

"Did you see Xilavela in the Zapotec altepetl?" said Naran

interrupting the frightened man whose eyes struggle trying to recall such a name. "The princess Xilavela?" said Naran, trying to make it clearer.

"There, there is no such person with that name"
Naran let go, unsure of what was going on, and looked at Quetzal, who responded to Naran's silent question. "Knowing Kinich Ahau, he probably found out what you are trying to do."

"He said I could gather all the information I wanted and said he would be waiting."

"Yes, the information. Not fix your eyesight and try to conceal me. Plus, he never said he would wait in the Zapotec altepetl." What Quetzal was saying made sense, but something was not right. Dismissing the Tecuhtli, he returned to the chantli he was staying in and began walking in circles, trying desperately to find an answer. While Quetzal stays silently in a corner watching how Naran becomes anxious and neurotic.

"The girl that helped us on the lake. Are you sure she was human?"

"Yes, I'm sure."

"And Xoaltentli?"

"Naran, I'm still partially connected with Kinich Ahau. If it was him, I would have recognized him."

"Then why didn't you tell me about Xilavela right away?"

"He looked like a human being. You recognize him right away, remember?"
For a moment, Naran felt dizzy and sat down on the floor. *Something is off. My head is hurting.*

"Breath Naran, breathe," said Quetzal, and then on the second breath, Naran fainted.

Chapter 20

Finding himself seated at the base of the Popocatepetl, not sure how he got there or when Naran stood up quickly, and his heart began to beat out of control.

"Sir?" Once again, Xoaltentli appeared out of nowhere, indicating he was dreaming.

"Who are you?" said Naran with a shivering voice that shows he was about to break.

"That's not important." Disoriented and scared, Naran went right to the neck of Xoaltentli. "I'm not going to harm you, sir."

"I don't know how you are doing this, Kinich Ahau, but I promise you are going to regret it."
Smiling, he pulls away quickly without trouble from Naran's grip. "It seems you are confusing me with someone else."

Frustration had reached its limit, and Naran felt tears sliding down his cheeks. "I'm losing my mind!"

Taking Naran's hand, he guided him to a tree and made him sit down "are you like this because of the answer you can't find?"

Naran's hands were shaking, making him feel weak. "I don't know anymore."

Placing his hand on Naran's hand, trying to calm him with a

small smile, "that's good." The look Naran gave suggested that he wasn't sure who was madder. "It's good that you have hit the end of this road. Now you would have to step back and see others," said Xoaltentli as an explanation to what he meant.

"I-I don't understand."

"Are you afraid of death?"

Naran looked at his hands and remembered all the blood and the lives he had taken. "At this point, all I want is to die."

Xoaltentli smiled again "if you are not afraid of death, why does it matter the answer or the question?"

The corners of Naran's lips moved upwards, showing a sad smile "because I wouldn't be the only one dying," and with that, Naran let out a cry that came from his heart. For a moment, he forgot he could feel things like pain.

"I see," said Xoaltentli patting Naran's back. It didn't matter if Xoaltentli was a friend or an enemy. Naran's mind had so many things that he had kept for so long that the only thing he could do at that moment was to let everything out.

"I think the problem you have is that you want to act tough and painless, but what you are doing is running away. Your mother's actual death, the way you had to live, the injustice and cruelty of your kind. It's valid that those things provoke genuine emotions like anger, sadness, and pain."

It didn't surprise Naran that Xoaltentli knew all that, especially his mother's death. "I don't want to feel any of that," said Naran, almost out of breath.

"Ah, see now the truth comes out. Feelings are part of being human and alive."

"But it hurts so much" Naran hit his chest repeatedly, then grabbed his clothes with such force that it seemed he wanted to rip his own heart out.

"Of course, it will hurt, so much so that you will probably die. Then it will pass, and you'll have to live, learning how to do everything again."

"I don't think I can do that."

"That's because you haven't tried it yet. You keep putting up a resistance, avoiding such emotions, is the reason why you are unable to move forward and find what you are looking for."

Naran took deep breaths, trying to calm himself to talk again "why are you telling me all this?"

"A time will come, and a decision must be made. If you are not ready, then all of this will go to waste" when Naran turns to face Xoaltentli, he finds himself alone, and again everything turns black.

Waking up to the sound of the birds, Naran's body aches, but his head seems clear and calm. He knew deep down that Kinich Ahau would never have such considerations with him and certainly not give him a heads up for what is coming. Although what Xoaltentli said didn't make sense, Naran felt different, as if he wasn't pretending to be brave anymore.

Recalling the conversation, he headed up to the Popocatepetl with Quetzal to ensure he wasn't dreaming. Quetzal did not question him, didn't ask if he was alright. He simply walked beside him in silence.

They walk for a while until they reach the same scenery of Naran's dream. "It's odd to see a tree up here" Quetzal's observation made Naran approach the tree, looking and touching every part. *There must be a reason why he appears only in this place,* Naran thought with the hope that a clue could be hiding somewhere.

The sun started to hide, and it was getting harder to see. "We should head back. There is nothing here, Naran," ignoring Quetzal. He kept digging around the tree after having turned over every texcalli. Then, when the full moon shone brightly in the night sky, silver paths began to form in the tree trunk, and all of them led to the middle, where slowly they started to compose words that led to a message.

'Start where your heart turned against you'

"That's a weird thing to say," said Quetzal, getting closer to the tree, making sure there weren't any other words. At the same time, Naran repeatedly said the words in his head, *'start where your heart turned against you.' The* problem was that Naran didn't remember when exactly that happened.

Feeling confused and useless, Naran walked back to the chantli in silence. Quetzal stood behind him, disguised with the night, waiting for him to talk and explain what was going on. He decided to lay down outside, admiring the xitlalli. "Why do I suddenly feel tired and sleepy?" said Naran rubbing his eyes, feeling some tears trap there

"I'm not sure either."

"Could it be that my human side is fighting?"

"Or maybe you were trying to prove yourself something and

went to the extreme."

The comment made Naran chuckle because Xoaltentli had suggested the same thing. "I'm starting to believe that there is a small chance that an Ometeotl exists, one that is not of your kind or mine. For some reason, this gives me a certain peace."

Quetzal said nothing and lay down next to Naran

"Where do you think Kinich Ahau is now?

"I don't know."

"didn't you say you were still connected with him?"

"As in, I can see through his disguise without knowing his location."

"Well, that's a useless thing."

"Glad you are in the mood to mock me."

Naran smiles and stretches his hands. "If this is the end, may as well enjoy it, don't you think?"

"What happened to the tree reminds me of someone," said Quetzal, ignoring what Naran said.

"Who?"

"Doesn't matter, he can be here" Naran could sense that Quetzal was thinking of something that troubled him, yet he knew that it's better not to pray and let him figure it out himself. In the end, Quetzal always shares his thoughts.

Unaware of when and where exactly did his heart turn against him, Naran decided to head back to his altepetl, starting where his mother died. Even though his head was full of painful memories, he felt free and at peace for the first time.

The strange dreams with Xoaltentli stop, which means one

of two things. First, that Naran was finally going in the right direction. Second, something terrible happened, and it was a matter of time before Kinich Ahau showed up. That thought led Naran to question the time frame he had to work with. If Kinich Ahau was waiting for him, this probably meant that he had more time than what was expected.

Chapter 21

Early morning right before the sunrise, Naran and Quetzal left. If everything went well and there were no wrong turns, they should be arriving in two days. Feeling he had an advantage, now that he had been traveling, encouraged him to believe there would be no problem to find the right road. He also had the Popocatepetl as a good point of reference. Among the stuff he might need, Naran included other weapons that didn't contain iztli. Deciding as well to avoid using the sword Kinich Ahau gave him. It's still a mystery to him the true purpose behind it, so it was best to refrain from using it.

Besides the bad memories, Naran had questions that he never considered before. Most of the things Xoaltentli said were hard to understand. All his life, things have been 'yes' or 'no,' 'death' or 'alive,' nothing in between, and no other option. Then Kinich Ahau appears with Quetzal, transforming everything he believes and proving wrong the knowledge his ancestors have taught. "Quetzal, how is it that you didn't know about reincarnation?"

The shadowy figure who has kept silent and walked behind Naran now catches up with him. "When Kinich Ahau and I fought, he kept me locked. He would let me out for a bit, but I don't recall much. Also, I couldn't go back to earth, at least not in the way I wanted"

Even if this was true, it did not explain why they ended up in this situation. "What was the actual reason for the fight?"

"We made a deal. Kinich Ahau would help me become human, and in return, I would get rid of a few people." He slowed down the pace. "Kinich Ahau lured another god and made him possess a human. Once inside, he kills the human, trapping the god. That's when I enter the body and become a human." He stopped talking. Naran could tell Quetzal was struggling. "It was my turn to do my part. Kinich Ahau handed me a blade, and... I don't remember how it started, but I recall seeing her next to Kinich Ahau" he took a deep breath "he betrayed me. I don't know how much she saw, but it was enough for her to walk away."

This made Naran feel that there was a connection. "Do you remember any detail in the sword?"

"No." There was not enough information to make any deductions. *Every time I feel closer to the truth, it turns into a dead end. Well, at least there was a good reason behind the fight. But it still seems unnecessary.* He stops and looks at Quetzal. "You could have come here like Kinich Ahau, right?"

"Yes"

"Then why-"

Guessing what Naran was going to say, Quetzal interrupted him to add, "as someone who lives an eternity, but I... I wanted to die with her. To grow old and die with her."

Naran chuckles at the hidden message Quetzal is given to him.

Then his face turns rigid, and without holding back, he says what he has been thinking for a while "you became greedy."

"It's not like that, Naran," said Quetzal in a defensive way.

"You wanted to be with her, and you were with her, but that wasn't enough. You wanted more. How is that not greedy?" Naran stops and turns to face Quetzal. "Why don't you start to face your truth instead of excusing your every action? You are a god, after all. What are you so afraid of?"

Quetzal kept silent. His eyes widen for a moment and then turn back to normal "disappointment."

"Need more than that"

"You are right. I was a god. I earned my place among the powerful ones. I was content with my life, and I walked into your realm many times before everything went downhill. Curiosity was part of the problem, as well as new emotions, but that wasn't all. I had moments where I felt superior to your kind and thought of all of you as a useless creation. The only human that mattered to me was her. The rest were obstacles. So, when I killed all those humans, I didn't feel a thing, but she saw me. And that look on her face. Her eyes showed fear, sadness, and disappointment. Made my perfect little world vanish."

Naran could tell this was true because Quetzal often showed arrogance and a big fat ego. However, some things he said were off "I thought everyone did the same thing over and over, and no one cares about anyone. So how and why did you earn your place?"

The corner on Quetzal's eyes lifted, giving an indication of a smile. "A war occurred a long time ago. Dark forces wanted to take over this realm. We were asked to fight and be rewarded afterward. I didn't know anything about killing or weapons, so I stayed put along with others." He sighs almost as if he had been telling this story many times that he has become tired of it. "Kinich Ahau approached me and said that this realm had a destiny, that it held the key to many things. Therefore, we needed to preserve it by fighting. He made me believe it was part of my job to secure such precious organisms. I did, and we won. My reward was to become as powerful as Kinich Ahau. Although nothing changed other than being able to enter this realm in my form."

"Does this mean that Ometeotl asked you to fight?"

"No, we don't know much about him. He never interferes. He vibrates differently than we do."

"So, it's a he then?"

"No, I said it that way to make it easier for you to understand. However, we don't know if it's a female or a male, and we never care. It's just someone that only says and does things when needed."

"Is it part of your kind?"

"Not sure."

"Didn't you say he kills all who broke the law?"

"Well, we can't be killed, so I assume he simply took them somewhere."

Naran touched his forehead feeling pain and frustration. "None of this makes sense to me. If you don't know what it is, never see it, yet somehow only speak to set rules and take the ones that break those rules. Why are you and Kinich Ahau still here?"

"I have asked myself that same question."

Naran sigh. "Then who asked you to fight?"

"The powerful ones. They said that something needed to be done because those dark forces would destroy us next if not. Although it was a simple formality because they didn't need us."

"This means that Kinich Ahau made you participate in that war and in reward give you the same amount of power he has?"

"Yes"

"Why?"

"He said, later on, he would need my help, so it would be best if I had the same amount of power as him."

Most of the questions Naran had about Quetzal and Kinich Ahau have been answered. But, nevertheless, the curiosity on this strange being grew "where was the Ometeotl when this happened?"

"Don't know, never thought of that."

"I thought the purpose of your kind was to learn from anything?"

"Learn things that have nothing to do with us."

Naran's mount dropped open for a second, then he composed himself. "I'm starting to doubt that you are an evolution of my kind," he said and then continued walking. "Wait, so if a god possesses a human and the human dies, the god gets trapped inside?"

"Not unless you use a special relic."

"And I'm guessing Kinich Ahau has it?"

Quetzal denied with a mention of his head. "That divine relic was destroyed along with the others when the rules were broken. The only relic that Kinich Ahau has is Lihtnao" he said the last words slowly and with a lower voice, almost as if he recalled something.

"It doesn't seem you are sure about this."

"No, I am. I am"

It seems he is hiding something from me. But, even with that thought, Naran decided to let it go. He knows firsthand what it feels like to remember painful memories, and he had been pushing Quetzal to the limit. "Do you think you could possess something else?" said Naran trying to change the mood.

"What do you mean?"

"When I met you, you looked like a serpent, so I thought maybe you could possess a real serpent and see what happens."

Quetzal chuckle "before Kinich Ahau gave me power, I was considered a low-rank god. When I came to earth the first time, your realm tried to give me an acceptable form. That's probably why your kind names me Quetzalcoatl."

"Either way, we could try."

"Naran, I know it's hard, but you need to accept it. I am going to die."

It was the first time they used the word 'die,' which made Naran feel horrible. "Thought gods can't die," he said, trying to lighten his mood.

"There is always a first time for everything."

"Then what if you could reincarnate just like humans?"

"Into what, a serpent?" said Quetzal in between laughter

"Maybe or maybe a human or something else entirely. That could be a possibility."

Quetzal sigh. "Naran, I'm not afraid of dying. If anything, I'm afraid of leaving you alone," he said, looking at Naran with a warm smile.

"There you go again, making things awkward" they both laugh and forget for a moment their miserable state.

"I wish things have been different for us," said Quetzal with a nostalgic tone

"Define different?"

He sighs before answering, "a place where we could be together without causing any harm."

Even though Naran does not feel the same love and affection for Quetzal as he does for Naran, he could relate. "If you would see her again, as you remember, what would you tell her?"

Quetzal's eyes seem glossy, almost as if he was about to cry. "That if I could turn back in time, I would have been with her till her death and reincarnation, not caring if she looks different every time because it will still be her." He pauses for a moment and turns to see Naran. "To my eyes, you are the most gorgeous being that could ever have existed."

Chapter 22

Slowly the sun hides behind the mountains, letting a few last rays of light hit Naran's feet, making him stop right outside his altepetl. *Maybe Tecuhtli is still around,* thought Naran and headed directly to the chantli of his former Tecuhtli. A thousand thoughts ramble around his head, nothing concrete and not a specific topic, making it hard to focus on what he will talk about or ask the Tecuhtli.

By the time they got there, all thoughts had died down. Before him, the chantli that once laid there was destroyed. Naran lost his temper for a moment and smashed the remindings of the chantli "breath Naran" Quetzal said, but he dismissed him. Trying to distract himself, he decided to enter the forest and gather wood for a campfire. He silently chopped the trees with the sword Kinich Ahau gave him, wanting to destroy it, but it did no damage. He picks up the small pieces of wood and starts to pile them on the side.

"Who wrote those words on the tree?" Quetzal watched Naran at a safe distance and decided to ask something that Naran didn't know. Either way, he kept silent about Xoaltentli.

"This place burned down a few days ago. It doesn't seem like a recent event," said Naran, trying to change the topic. "Do you think Kinich Ahau did this?"

"No, he doesn't care enough to have done this"

Then Naran remembers that there was a small group out there taking down the rest of the altepetl. *Maybe Kinich Ahau sent them. Does this mean that he also knew about Xoaltentli?*

"Naran, who wrote those words on the tree?"

"I don't know Quetzal. If I knew who or what it was, I would feel more reassured of this trip."

They went back to silence after that. Naran sat down in front of the campfire. The heat slowly reached his hands. He looks at them and touches the scars and calluses. *I was human once.*

"You still are, Naran."

"Can you stay away from my thoughts?"

Quetzal chuckles as his eyes shine more than usual, probably the reflection of the fire. "The important thing is that you understand that your humanity will remain until you decide to forget it. When you forget then, probably, you will end up like Kinich Ahau and me."

"Which is worse because you are not human," said Naran with a smile.

This makes Quetzal glare at him, "we might not be human, but we do recognize what does it mean to take care of others...or at least we used to."

It became a habit for Naran to push Quetzal to the limit. However, the discussion only made him remember his situation "it doesn't matter anymore. Kinich Ahau's actions made me believe his plan is already done, and he is just waiting for us to catch up."

"probably"

Naran lay back, admiring the night sky full of xitlalli. Once again, his head became full of information that he couldn't fully grasp.

The warmth of the rays of sun hitting Naran's face woke him up. Surprisingly he was feeling things now, including hunger. Getting up and searching for the right tool, he went to a river nearby to get some fish. Feeling full again made him smile. *Maybe I'm not a lost cause after all.* He cleaned up, trying to avoid leaving evidence that might let people know they were there.

"Where to now?" said Quetzal as he watches Naran

"Teotihuacan"

Quetzal turns to face Naran, his eyes showing worry. "I don't think it is a good idea for you to see that place."

"Good or not, that's the next place where my heart did things blindfolded," and that was enough for Quetzal to support Naran's choices without complaining.

Dark thoughts started to invade Naran's head as they walked in silence, eyes fixed on the road. The exact route they traveled with Kinich Ahau the first time. The sound of screams and the smell of burning skin consume him, making him stop and close his eyes.

Rushing to Naran, worried that he might faint once more, Quetzal said, "Naran, let's stop for today."

"No, we still have a long way to go."

"If you keep this up it-"

"Quetzal, we need to continue," said Naran dismissing Quetzal's attempts to safeguard him. Taking a deep breath gathering all his strength, he kept walking. When they reached the entrance, Naran's heart beat faster than usual. Seeing the soundless altepetl cover by night create such a painful memory that his eyesight became blurry. "Quetzal, let's rest here" Naran drops down to the floor.

Quetzal rested his shadowy hand on Naran's shoulder. "Everything will be fine" was the last thing Naran heard before the blackness surrounded him.

Opening his eyes finding himself standing at the top of the main teôcalli in the Teotihuacan altepetl

"Beautiful isn't" once more, Xoaltentli was standing next to Naran with a bright smile.

"People were sacrificed here," said Naran sitting on the edge.

"Don't let that event overshadow the beauty of this place. It took a lot of effort to be constructed."

Naran sat there looking at the entire land that surrounded the teôcalli "it's hard."

"What's hard?"

"To see more than the damage."

Xoaltentli sat next to Naran and said, "that is because you are only focusing on the wound, not on what it created" Naran turned to Xoaltentli. It didn't require him to speak for Xoaltentli to explain further "every hardship is necessary. How many tlalolin do you think were needed for the Popocatepetl to be what it is right now? Even the chiauitl needs to die to become a papalotl."

Although it made sense what Xoaltentli was saying, for Naran, it was an excuse "killing humans is wrong and unnecessary."

"But the only way for you to find out that it was 'wrong and unnecessary' was by doing it. Otherwise, you would never question yourself with those thoughts."

Naran gave a small and weak smile "are you saying killing is alright?"

"No, I'm saying that by acting, you are learning what is right and wrong. There are things that you don't have to do to see and understand that that's not the way, for example, sacrifices."

Feeling that he was actually speaking with Ometeotl made it a rare opportunity to know the truth his heart was seeking. "Then why don't you do something about it? Why do you let bad things happen?" said Naran.

Xoaltentli smiled warmly as he always did. "Everyone is free to do whatever they want, and every action they take has consequences. How can I undo a wrong that was created by a human free will? Don't you think that the only ones that can change something are the same people who made it?"

Naran sigh having the feeling that he always had with Xoaltentli, the sense of learning something more significant than him. "But there is nothing I can do to fix this. I have killed so many people. This entire altepetl perishes by my hand, and... the children."

"You are not supposed to fix anything."

"Then?"

"Naran, all those people are gone. They all left, not knowing why their time has come. They did not care who killed them; rather, they cared what they could not tell their loved ones" Xoaltentli locks eyes with Naran as he continues, "you are the only one condemning yourself. Before you assume, I am not saying that what you did was right or that it wasn't your fault. I'm trying to tell you that what is done is done, and nothing can change that. Forgive yourself and ask for forgiveness. Clean the earth, make it fertile again for new flowers to grow."

"Is this going to help me defeat Kinich Ahau?"

"Do you think defeating him will change anything?" The question took Naran by surprise. He never thought of what was going to happen once Kinich Ahau was gone.

"Why did you want me to come here?" said Naran avoiding answering Xoaltentli's question

"Is very simple. If you want to move forward, you need to heal your wound, and the only way to do that is by facing yourself. Confront your fears Naran" Xoaltentli stood up and stayed on the very edge of the teôcalli. This was an indication that their conversation had ended and Naran was going to soon wake up. "Just remember that someone will always remain alive," and with that, he disappears, not allowing Naran to ask what he meant by that.

Waking up early in the morning, Naran walks to the teôcalli, hoping to find another clue. As he reached the stairs, the memories of that horrible night made him bent down in pain.

"Naran, if you keep this up, you-"

"How about you encourage me instead of wanting me to give

up?"

Quetzal tried to help him stand, but it was useless. He was no longer solid. Naran noticed this and became alarmed for a moment, then took a deep breath and stood up "let's reach the top, then we will figure out what to do" slowly, they continued. Every step brought Naran painful memories. It was starting to be harder and harder. Each time he took a breath, he said to himself, *I can do nothing, so please forgive me.* When they reached the top, Naran noticed he was sweating even though the sun started to feel less intense.

Quetzal approached him and stood in front of him, "Naran, I don't think I have much time left."

"There has to be something here that can-"

"Naran, maybe I wasn't supposed to continue."

"What are you saying?"

"I was supposed to die a long time ago, and thanks to Kinich Ahau, I kept breathing. It was probably to see you again and be able to make amends with you."

"Quetzal, please," begging him to stay, begging him to fight, "just hold a bit more," said Naran

"Listen to me, last night while you were asleep, I found a passage, a hiding place under the teôcalli. I noticed it has a special force, almost like the portal we use to come to your realm. Be careful and don't do anything rash. Always remember to breathe-"

"Stop! Please stop! I can't-"

"Naran, listen to me! This was never my journey" the shadowy figure was turning into a foggy mist. "Even though I would not be there with you when you defeat Kinich Ahau, I'm sure you would do a great job. I believe in you" Quetzal's hand reached Naran's cheek. "Never forget who you are and never forget how much I love you," eyes full of tears with a whimpering heart. Naran begs silently for a moment to catch up with what was happening. However, the sun kept its course, and as it did, so did Quetzal. Before he was gone entirely, the shadowy figure put his arms around Naran to hold one last time. *I don't know who you see in your dreams, but please don't assume it is someone who cares about you.* Said Quetzal just before he vanished.

The moon shone brighter than the sun ever did. Naran had been on his knees for what seemed a long time. His heartfelt numbness as well as his entire body. Quetzalcoatl was the second person who showed him love; that reminded him what to do and what not to do; that cared for his well-being. Now he, too, is gone. Making him feel the same way he did when his mother took her life to protect him. *I never asked you to die for me. I never wanted their sacrificial love.* Feeling the anger reaching new horizons and unable to hold it anymore, he screamed. A light engulfed his body, and a blazing blue fire poured from him into the sky. Not able to keep it anymore, he fell down, hitting the hard floor. *Please just kill me, be done with me,* he thought as he drifted into darkness.

Chapter 23

Days and nights pass. The rain came and went, making the floor cold. Life went on, yet for Naran, time had stopped. Strength left his body, so he remained on the floor unmoved. His mind felt empty and quiet. Never noticed the space Quetzal took in his mind until he was gone. The silence was all that he had and a persistent huitzilin that kept fluttering around him.

"Sir?" The voice of Xoaltentli made Naran think that at some point, he had gone to sleep. Aside from that, he remains unaffected. "Nothing would bring him back." Xoaltentli bent down, moving a stray hair from Naran's face. "You have to learn to live again." Naran gazed at Xoaltentli. He couldn't understand how the earth would keep up going as if nothing happened. "It seems you forgot what I told you about death." Naran shrugs, unable to recall anything. "He is still out there."

"How?" said Naran with a rusty voice.

Smiling, proud of poking Naran's curiosity, Xoaltentli answers him, "in a different realm, one that you cannot access, not yet."

Getting up in a sitting position, surprised he could feel his sore muscles. "Was there a way to save him?" he said with a hope that by now, it was useless.

"What makes you think he needed saving?"

"You know what I meant"

The hint of exasperation on Naran's last comment made Xoaltentli smile more openly. "What difference does it make? It won't change what happened" he then sat next to Naran.

"Because I-"

"Because you will have an excuse to feel remorseful and blame yourself to the point of you becoming the victim of this situation?" Naran kept silent, knowing deep down that what Xoaltentli said was precisely what would end up happening. "Humans have a tendency of forgetting that everything happens the way it's supposed to. Every step you take has a consequence, and when that consequence is not in your favor, you regret it and get hooked on the 'what if.' That's when you become a victim of your own guilt, non-existent guilt, if I may add."

Every word this boy has told Naran since day one was a mystery to him "Xoaltentli, I don't have the proper brain to understand half of what you say."

He chuckled, "Alright, let me put it differently, everything that happens is perfect, and there was no other way it could have been done. That was the only way, and that way was perfect. Does this make more sense to you?"

"No, but thanks for trying," said Naran, remembering the last thing Quetzal told him.

"Well, I tried," said Xoaltentli, in between laughter. It was the first time Naran heard him laugh, and it was so clean and pure, very different from Kinich Ahau.

"Why are you in such a good mood?"

"I am always in a good mood. Maybe you haven't noticed because every time we meet, you have thoughts rambling."

Agreeing with him, feeling the pain of a loss all over again. Although he was thankful that death made his thoughts leave for a moment, "I couldn't say goodbye. He died thinking that what happened to me all those lifetimes ago was his fault."

"Lifetimes?"

"Yes, you know, when you die and come back as a different person."

"I know what lifetimes mean," Xoaltentli chuckled. "What I was trying to say was 'your lifetimes?'"

"Well, yes, my lifetimes."

"Naran, this is your first life."

"What?"

Xoaltentli clear his throat before talking again "this life right now, this is your first one, although the concept of lifetimes might not be used correctly because it-"

"Wait, no, that is not possible. Kinich Ahau showed me my past lives. He showed them to me."

"Nobody can 'show you' your past lives. That's a personal journey."

That makes sense. "Then?" said Naran

"Then what?"

"Xoaltentli!"

"Naran"

"Explain!"

"What?"

Getting up, passing his hands through his hair, frustrated by Xoaltentli behavior. *Is he acting like this on purpose?* "You know what I mean" Xoaltentli looked up at Naran with a question mark in his eyes. "What did Kinich Ahau show me then?" said Naran elaborating more on what he meant

"Probably his memories."

"How is that possible?"

Xoaltentli shrugged with a smirk on his lips that made Naran lose his temper. "Who the fuck are you?!" he said, which was not what he intended to say. Maybe he had been thinking that for a while, and spur of the moment, he said it out loud.

"No one, I am simply a witness," said Xoaltentli with such calmness that only made things worse for Naran.

However, his mind became busy processing the new information. He had no space for anger. "If this is my first life and those memories that Kinich Ahau showed me were not me, then who-" stopping mid-sentence when the images of the eyes rush back at him, all at once, creating a sharp pain. "My mother!"

"Where?"

"That was my mother's eyes. He was showing me my mother's past lives," said Naran ignoring the lack of interest in Xoaltentli

"no one can show you-"

"I know, I know...so this means that he was there with her all her life. Did Quetzal know about this?"

"Does it matter?"

"Well, no, but he, he died thinking I was her"

"I don't think so."

"What makes you say that?"

"Everyone passes through enlightenment when their soul leaves their body, so probably he realized you were not her. By the way, who are you talking about?"

"My mother"

"oh"

Sudden happiness covered Naran's body for a second, then fury overtook him. "That bastard, how could he do this?!"

"Who? Me?"

"No, Kinich Ahau."

"Oh well, that I don't know."

"You are very irritating today." Xoaltentli shrugs again. "When do I wake up?" said Naran with a hint of urgency

"You are awake."

"So, I'm able to speak with you anytime now?"

"No, you are hallucinating from the lack of sleep and food. There is a river nearby. You should go and have some water." Noticing that Xoaltentli walks behind him, Naran rushes down and heads to the river.

The heat of the campfire warmed Naran's hands, who sat in silence watching the light of the flames reflected on Xoaltentli's eyes "why are you still here?"

"Do you want me to leave?"

"No, it's just...weird that I can still see you. I feel like I'm asleep."

"Rest assured; you are awake."

Then they stay in silence, giving Naran a moment to think about the next steps he would have to undertake. So far, he had been trying to save Quetzal, and now that that is over, he wasn't sure how to approach Kinich Ahau.

"This might be the last time we will see each other," said Xoaltentli unexpectedly.

Bringing Naran back to the present, unsure of what he meant by that "why?" Xoaltentli shrugged again. Even though he is a strange character, today, he was acting more bizarre. Feeling curious and wanting to know more, Naran remembered that because of 'curiosity,' disaster occurred.

Planning was not Naran's strong suit. Every single one up until now had failed. The last hope lay on this secret passage, although Naran didn't have high hopes. Xoaltentli left in the morning, making Naran feel that he wasted an opportunity to question him about many things. Either way, he was grateful for all the things Xoaltentli had taught him, even if there was a possibility that everything was a lie or a trap. However, what bothered him the most was that he realized how alone he used to be. When his mother died, he dived into work, then Kinich Ahau appeared with Quetzal, and all these people made him feel the warmth of company.

Suppressing his emotions, he walked to the hidden passage Quetzal mentioned after leaving. He found the strange narrow entrance on the side of the main teôcalli. It took him more time than expected to enter the place. *How did Quetzal find this place?* He thought as he slipped and fell for the tenth time. The site seemed to have suffered a collapse that made Naran believe if this was his doing. He had to crawl a few times, primarily because of the absence of light. He wasn't sure of where he was and if it was safe enough to walk normally.

Thousands of tiny twinkling lights spread throughout the roof. A cold breeze and no other light sources made Naran believe that somehow, he exited the cave and was now standing under the night sky. *Where am I exactly?* Stretching his hands, he could feel a rough and small piece of something hard, which meant that the twinkling lights were simple texcalli. *But why do they shine like that?* His question went numb when he felt a powerful pull from the center of the cave. *Quetzal said this place was a portal similar to the one they use to travel through realms. Could this be a portal to their world?* With that thought in mind, he took a step forward.

Everything spun around, and he began to feel his feet leave the floor. The sensation of having no ground under him caused his heart to beat rapidly. The cold invaded his skin, making him scream in pain as he felt his bones and brain pulled in all directions and, at the same time, being squeezed.

After what felt like an eternity, he plunged, hitting water instead of ground. Gasping for air, desperately trying to find the way out, he swam around hopelessly, unsure where up was. *I need to calm down, just calm down, Naran!* Slowly his mind became clear, and he noticed the fake twinkling xitlalli that gave him a sense of direction.

Laying on the ground, breathing slowly, conscious of his surroundings and oblivious to how he got there yet aware that he was no longer in the Teotihuacan altepetl. "I knew it was you," the voice gave Naran chills. Closing his eyes, begging to be wrong. Even after doing a silent prayer, everything proved ineffective, as he opened his eyes, finding Kinich Ahau standing in front of him. "Come on, let's get you out of here" Kinich Ahau tried to help Naran. Yet, he pushed the god aside and got up by himself. Walking towards an arch, the only place that had light and stepping out, he found himself at the base of a teôcalli with two texcalli in the form of a serpent head. "Quetzal might have been their inspiration."

Naran turns to see Kinich Ahau. "Did you kill everyone here as well?"

"Some ran, others took their lives, but that's irrelevant."
I wish I had the sword this moment. Tiny specks of light began to form in his hand, making the sword appear out of thin air. Naran smiled —he was no longer in shock when incredible things happened.

He pointed the blade right in Kinich Ahau's throat "easy Naran."

"Quetzal died because of you. As a matter of fact, a lot of people died because of you."

"You mean because of us."

"If you want it that way, yes, because of us" Naran pressed the sword against his skin, making Kinich Ahau step back. "My life was ruined because of you" with a victory smile, he continued,

"Found something that can hurt you," said Naran.

He swung the sword and aimed at the head "so you're going to kill me like you killed your mother?"

"Don't you dare mention her!"

"I am only telling the truth."

Naran kept the sword close to the god's face "the past lives you show me, they are not about me. Those were my mother's past lives."

To which Kinich Ahau smiles, "well done. How did you figure it out?"

Ignoring what Kinich Ahau said, Naran continued saying, "there is one thing I want to know before I end your life." He lowered the sword. "Why me?" he said and waited for the answer.

"Because you are my child."

Naran chuckled. "Why can you be honest for once?"

Kinich Ahau disappears and appears behind Naran, grabbing the sword's grip, pushing Naran aside. "I am not lying." The sword began to tremble. Small orbs of light started to emerge from the point of the blade.

There were so many that soon they were surrounded by them. "What are those things?"

"Souls" the souls began to move and gather in Kinich Ahau palm "Aren't they beautiful."

"Whose souls, are they?"

"You gather them for me."

"Are you telling me that those are the souls of all the people I have killed"

"Yes. As you know, we are not able to handle the iztli. I tried innumerable times, but it never worked"

Then Naran remembered what Kinich Ahau said, "how can you be my father?"

"Your mother and I one night started to-"

"I mean, how is it possible for one of your kind to produce

offspring with a human?"

"We are not so different from humans."

Tears started to fall down. "Why my mother?"

"Quetzal loved her."

"You destroy her life just because of that?"

"I didn't destroy her life. If I recall correctly, you are the one who killed her."

Naran launched at Kinich Ahau with such anger that he desired nothing else but his death. With his hands around the god's neck, Naran was ready to end him "so you are planning to kill both of your parents?" That simple comment made Naran lose his grip enough for Kinich Ahau to escape. "I also needed someone to hold Quetzal," he whispers in Naran's ear.

"What?" said Naran stepping out of his touch

"He is or was a powerful being, every time I put him inside of a person, their body exploded. After many times, I figured that one of our own could survive, but they also died. Then your mother had a brilliant idea to pray for a baby. That's when it hit me" he sounded so cheerful and unaffected by the situation that made Naran feel this whole thing was fake.

"Why did you need Quetzal inside someone?"

"To be consumed. If I let him loose, he would have stopped me. I couldn't have that" Naran's head turn in circles feeling dizzy "careful there, Naran," said the god approaching Naran, trying to hold him in "why don't we sit down?" He pushed the god away, but he was too weak. Darkness began to surround him.

Chapter 24

Finding himself sitting at the top of a foreign teôcalli with the bright sun in front of him made Naran think that everything had been a dream. *How can it be a dream if it feels so real? Every aspect of that place was so detailed and unknown that it's impossible, I imagine.* Thought Naran feeling on edge

"isn't beautiful" Xoaltentli's voice startles Naran making him stand up rapidly, thinking it was Kinich Ahau.

"Why are you here?"

He simply shrugs and walks towards Naran with a compassionate look on his face. "So, what is bothering you this time?" How Xoaltentli spoke as he always did in dreams made Naran wonder if what happened with Kinich Ahau is real. If this is correct, then he had to gather as much information as possible before going back to the god "I am sure you are aware of what that sword holds." Xoaltentli sat on the edge of the teôcalli, his feet hanging, then turned to Naran with an invitation to sit next to him. "Why don't you tell me what you saw?"

Taking a deep breath ignoring the sensation that something was off, he said, "Kinich Ahau told me he was my father and that all those people I killed, their souls trapped on the sword, and he said he needed me to get rid of Quetzal and he choose my mother just because Quetzal love her and-"

"Breath Naran."

Which he did, and tears started to float down "it all happened so quickly."

Placing a hand on Naran's back, a gesture that never bothered him until now. With a serene face, he said, "this is how they usually look, a foreshadowing of a future event."

"What's foreshadowing?" *Quetzal warned me not to trust him, so why do I keep doing what he says? Worst, why do I keep believing his words?* Naran thought and began to feel the danger approaching.

"Something that hasn't happened yet eventually, it will."

"Then it is true, he is my father and, and" Naran began to hyperventilate, feeling his head with all sorts of thoughts that lead him to want to die.

"Let the pain absorb you, don't fight it. It will soon be over." To Naran's body, what Xoaltentli said felt like an order that he couldn't refuse. He took a deep breath and, with it, all the pain.

His eyes felt on fire —and he was not mistaken for a sudden light escaping them. A fire ring replaced his iris and his body levitated for a few seconds, although for Naran, it felt ages. Because while he was in the air, everything seemed strange and surreal. For a moment, he saw Quetzalcoatl not as a shadow but as a man. A man with delicate features, kind eyes, and surprisingly short hair, with a strong body that resembles nothing like a shadow. It amazes Naran how a god like that could be reduced to a fragile thing with nothing but a pair of eyes. *Naran.*

Said the god with a voice he thought he would never hear again. *Don't alter the reality as you did your mother's death. Face it.* Then every decision he has taken since the moment he took his first breath rushed down on him, waking him up.

The sounds of thousands of birds with other noises that he couldn't comprehend which animal was making them. Sitting down, feeling texcalli and dirt as if it was the first time, he felt such things. "Beautiful, isn't it?" The voice of Xoaltentli danced in Naran's ears with such intensity that he was able to taste the words for a moment.

"What happened?"

"Your unconscious and conscious align."

As his eyes focused, he noticed the bright face of Xoaltentli, that for some reason it reminded him of the gods he had encountered. "You are not the Ometeotl, are you?" he asked.

Xoaltentli smiles mischievously without answering. And with that simple gesture, everything falls apart. Naran kept recalling the so-called 'foreshadowing' and everything that Xoaltentli had told him since day one. Some things made perfect sense, yet something seemed out of place. A piece was missing. He had to keep his posture, avoiding raising any suspicion, so he sat in silence, watching the sun go down slower than usual. Even the clouds seem unhurried. The breeze caresses his face, making him feel a warm hug that reminds him he is not alone.

Since he is now aligned, the scenery before him astonishes him. Feeling momentary that he is witnessing another realm made matters worse. *This had to be the dream*, yet it felt natural. *One has to be false*. The presence of Xoaltentli dispels the thought of death. Then feeling the cold stone beneath him prompted him to the present and made him realize he is still on the top of the Teotihuacan teôcalli. *This is not another realm, then.* "Why does he need souls?" said Naran trying to gain time and information while he figures out what exactly is going on

"They become energy, and whoever absorbs them gains power," answers Xoaltentli calmly.

Apparently, being greedy is a normal state for every god, including Quetzal. "Isn't Kinich Ahau the most powerful being here?"

"In this realm, yes, but not in others" the way he responded so casually, gazing at Naran now and then, made Naran wary.

He must sense I am not buying his good intentions "what happens to those souls once he consumes the energy?"

Turning to face Naran with a severe face, Xoaltentli said, "they cannot reincarnate, nor move on."

"isn't the same thing?"

The usual smile appeared on Xoaltentli's lips. For some reason, it made Naran feel safe. "Humans need to find the purpose of their existence through lessons and hardships. The problem is that they usually run from the pain instead of accepting it and learning from it" he stops to chuckle, almost as if he remembers something in mid-sentence. "There are some that cling to that pain because they confuse it with happiness or sometimes that pain gives them comfort so thinking of letting go...well let's just say they don't dare to do so. That's why they keep coming back. Each life is better than the last until they reach their truth."

"That's horrible," said Naran, mortified by such a thing. *It's an endless circle of torture.*

Xoaltentli laughs at the face of Naran that shows the struggle he was having of assimilating such a concept "then there are humans like you that on their first life can get it."

"To get what?"

He stood up while saying, "you stop running and let the pain consume you."

"That's because you help me out," said Naran, feeling the need to get on the good side of Xoaltentli.

"True, but it was up to you to continue fighting or surrender." *That's because you didn't give me any other choice.* Thought Naran as he got up. "There is a whole universe that humans ignore."

At this point, every fiber in Naran became alert. He had ignored the sense of something being wrong because Xoaltentli provided him with attention. Once again, his shortcomings made him an easy target. Having to improve his acting, he asked with curiosity, "Is the universe miaccîtlalli?"

"Sometimes I forget who I am talking with," said Xoaltentli bursting into laughter "miaccîtlalli is what you call the night sky with all those xitlalli. The universe is greater than that and is known as an invisible force, like air. You can feel it and only see it when it touches the tree leaves. To make it clear in this explanation, the tree leaves represent your kind and any other kind."

"So can the universe decide to avoid helping others?" said Naran playing along

"It works differently" he stopped again with a severe face that made Naran relax as he noticed Xoaltentli was trying to find the right words "Let's go back to the air. This exists without thinking if it helps you breathe or not. It simply exists. It's up to you to inhale or not. And if you use it wisely, it can dry your clothes or fan the fire."

"So, the universe made the foreshadowing that-"

"No. The foreshadowing helped you see that if you had destroyed Kinich Ahau, all those trapped souls would have been lost. This would have gone against your exact wishes. You want to help undo a wrong, and you cannot undo something by doing it with wrong intentions" he sighs and then continues. "The universe guided your every step to this moment. Still, it did not create the foreshadowing."

Naran knew precisely what the universe was because when he was in the state of alignment, he could taste it with the tip of his tongue. This was the only subject he could use to verify how much of what Xoaltentli says is true or false. Thankfully he gave a piece of information that made clear one thing, he is a god, and the foreshadowing was his doing. Although this only made matters worse for Naran, now he doubted everything that happened with Kinich Ahau. "I still can't understand a word you are saying," said Naran, hiding his new knowledge.

Xoaltentli sighs defeated, giving Naran a pat on his back "don't worry about it," believing Naran's little act.

To prevent Xoaltentli from doubting Naran's loyalty, he followed all orders and trained continuously with his newly acquired abilities. They were only suitable for making it easier to kill someone. And it's only possible if it's a human because, according to Xoaltentli, there is no way to kill a god nor extinguish his light unless he is imprisoned.

Xoaltentli's plan is that before Kinich Ahau gathers all the souls, Naran traps him. One way to do this is by trapping him in a human body just like Quetzalcoatl. The second one is to put him in the top of the Chichen Itza that contains a special force, strong enough to enclose a god.

When Naran asks about why the Chichen Itza has this special force? Xoaltentli answers vaguely by guessing that it could be the number of sacrifices and huentli done on it and the underground cenote, where Naran landed on the foreshadowing. However, if this was true that many other teôcalli would be the same.

Unsatisfied with the response Naran tried another route "How come the Chichen Itza has texcalli made in the form of a serpent?"

"I am sure you are aware that Quetzalcoatl appeared many centuries ago."

"Yes, but it doesn't explain why the Mayan altepetl created an entire teôcalli to honor Quetzal."

Xoaltentli simply shrugged and continued explaining to Naran how to make objects appear like when he summoned his sword in the foreshadowing event. Nevertheless, all that Naran cared about was the genuine intentions Xoaltentli had. *What's the need to train the ability to crush a human's heart with a simple motion of the hand and willpower if it's useless against a god? Why does he avoid talking about Quetzal's interaction in the human world?*

This question made Naran feel anxious and on guard worried that Xoaltentli decided to attack him.

Early in the morning, they walk towards the entrance of the secret passage in the Teotihuacan teôcalli. Once inside the underground cave, knowing that only he is leaving, Naran decided to risk it "last time you said we would not see each other again."

"I said maybe because I wasn't sure you were going to survive the foreshadowing," Xoaltentli said, smiling brightly.

Yet this only made Naran feel in danger. "You send me there not caring if I die?"

"Things must be done if we want to destroy Kinich Ahau" his eyes gave off a dark aura.

"I guess you are right. Thank you for everything," said Naran in a hurry, alarmed by Xoaltentli's reaction. He parted without looking back, hoping that Xoaltentli didn't follow him.

Chapter 25

This time around, expecting the pull in all directions, Naran could endure it. He holds his breath with anticipation just in time for him to land on water. Clearing his mind and staying calm at all times, he got out.

The last time he was in this cenote, he noticed a few resemblances to Quetzal form. Having the opportunity to be there again, he wandered around, finding what seemed to be chantli of different sizes and shapes, which could mean that people used to live there. Although, for Naran, it appears that this was a hideout from something —or someone. There were also a couple of texcalli with the form of a serpent. Their position made it seem this place was meant to be a huentli to —what Naran guessed— the god Quetzalcoatl.

"Thought it was you" the charismatic voice of Kinich Ahau didn't surprise him this time.

"Who was Quetzal?" said Naran while bending down to touch one of the texcalli.

The laughter of Kinich Ahau echoed throughout the cave. "He has been on earth many times before your mother came into sight." He stood next to Naran and continued. "Also, I did a few experiments once he was reduced to a shadow" he took a piece of texcalli and reduced it to a smidge.

"Experiment?" Naran asks with curiosity, standing up to be at Kinich Ahau's level

"I needed him to be held by a human for my plan to work. However, many of them died in the process. The Mayan altepetl was the only one who saw him as what he is. They built this tzacualli in his honor. The temple of KuKulkan."

"KuKulkan?" said Naran, ignoring for a moment his desire to learn more about the experiments Kinich Ahau was conducting.

"They gave him that name," looking around the cave with a particular disdain. "Each altepetl has their way of calling us," he smiles. "It's a very human thing to name everything."
Nostalgia filled Naran's chest, making him feel the pain that only memories can give "he never mentioned this to me," his words sounded normal. Yet, anyone could see how alone he was feeling.

"Ah, that's because I erase his memory each time," emptiness showed in his eyes. "Poor thing," he said, making Naran clenched his hands to withhold his anger.

Breathing slowly, he tries to calm himself before doing something he could regret later. They stood there for a moment, in total silence, with the occasional drop of water that hit the texcalli. Naran could feel a tingling sensation that came from Kinich Ahau "I assume you already know who you are and who I am." Naran nodded and began to walk towards the exit. Once outside, he took in Chichen Itza and all the steps he had to take.
"Is he completely gone?" ask Kinich Ahau with a hint of remorse, making Naran question for a moment if this god was actually

regretting his actions.

"Who? Quetzal? Yes, he disappeared a few days ago."

"Did you tell him?" He paused, almost doubting if he should continue "that the woman he loved was your mother and not you?" He finished without looking at anyone, just the ground. Naran denied with a slight motion of his head and began taking each step of the stairs.

The way Kinich Ahau is acting made everything confusing. Naran couldn't stop wondering if there was something else, he wasn't aware of because he could tell that Kinich Ahau was feeling guilty. However, past experience has shown not to trust any god. *None of that would matter if I had a slight chance of succeeding. And if I failed, at least I would die knowing I tried everything.*

The steps seem endless, and with the sun beginning to set, Naran could feel the eyes of Kinich Ahau and the energy that emanates from them. Strangely he could feel it flowing through his body as if it was part of him. "Seems I overestimated you." Kinich Ahau changed positions right when Naran was about to reach the top. He stood in front of Naran, "but I am curious about something" with a quick motion, he grabbed him by the neck. "Who told you of our blood relationship?"

"Does it matter now?" said Naran with difficulty. Kinich Ahau's gaze penetrated Naran's head to the point that it was impossible to hide something from him. Quickly Naran pushed him with an enormous strength making him fly and hit the front of the tzacualli, giving Naran time to catch his breath. Standing in front of the entrance where he needed to put Kinich Ahau, he grabbed him, putting his hands on his back and forcing him inside.

"Haven't you learned anything?" the god smirked, and suddenly Naran's hands did not respond to him. "Just because someone treats you kindly doesn't mean their intentions are pure" Kinich Ahau became free.

"What are you talking about?" ask Naran, knowing fully well what he meant and who he was referring to.

"It surprises me. Xoaltentli was able to hide when I annihilate all the gods" his shoulders relax as he continues, "well, I did leave a few that I needed." For a brief moment, his expression darkens. "He was definitely not one of them."

"You were the one that hunted them down?" Naran felt his mind collapsing and his heart agitated.

Kinich Ahau approaches Naran "aren't you lucky? Not even Quetzal knew about this," taking Naran's head. "If you got this far with Xoaltentli's help, then it means he is probably after the same thing." Naran could feel the same pull that meant Kinich Ahau was getting inside his mind and manipulating his body. "Give me the sword."

Both of them were so engaged and focused on not dying that they didn't notice the presence of someone else until it was too late. Everything stops. Naran feels a tug from his belly button and then loses all sensations. His body lifts into a dark sky with dancing lights surrounding him, "Naran," the voice made Naran's eyes open wide. His heartache "my beautiful son" the lights began to form a silhouette of a woman that Naran thought he would never see again. She embraces him in a warm hug as he begins to cry like a child.

"I don't know what to do," he said in between sobs.

"The mistakes we have made brought so much burden to you" she held him tight against her chest. Naran could feel himself relax and be able to breathe again. However, he noted that a heartbeat was missing in his mother's chest.

The times he had seen or heard his mother was in his memories, his subconscious. No god he had encountered so far could have done such a thing, except for one. *Xoaltentli,* he took the sword out and slew his supposed mother, hoping that would end the trick.

Founding himself back on Chichen Itza with his mind revolving, unable to focus, he could hear the two gods discussing. "Since when you became this powerful," said Kinich Ahau, out of breath. *Did Xoaltentli put him in the same state as me?* Thought Naran as he watched for the first time drops of sweat in Kinich Ahau's forehead

"You could say I was also busy," gazing at Xoaltentli, Naran notices that he had blood dripping from his chest where he slew his fake mother. But Xoaltentli seems to ignore his wound. *If they can't resist the iztli. How come he is not collapsing in pain?*

"I should have known it was you who sent Tezcatlipoca to the Olmec tribe." This piece of information made Naran realize that he was being used by another god from the beginning. Nevertheless, it's useless now. *This won't undo the past.*

"Never would I have thought you would continue trying to hold Quetzalcoatl," said Xoalentli, breathing slowly.

"And how did you find out?" Responded Kinich Ahau as he regained his superior posture.

"I met the kid and Quetzal by the river. Of course, I look different." He said, looking at Naran with a smile. *The girl in the river was him!* "Thanks to Naran and his weak mind, I was able to figure out your little game."

Back then, when Quetzalcoatl interacted with his mother, it nearly ended humankind. From that moment on, it has been a continuous intrusion from these so-called gods. Now once again, two powerful gods of a world that surpass Naran's compression fight for souls that should not belong to anyone. Thinking of this gave him the strength he needed to do whatever it takes to send them back to where they belong.

Gathering all his strength and courage, Naran launches with full force, hoping he was right about Xoaltentli mortality. "Careful, Naran, we can't die that easily," said Xoaltentli, a bit surprised by the attack.

Suppressing the urge to summon his sword, knowing the god's soul could be trapped in it, Naran grabs Xoaltentli by the neck "gods can't, but you are no god," he said.

"Stop!" ignoring Kinich Ahau, Naran put in use his new ability. With his free hand crushes Xoaltentli's heart effortlessly.

A bright light blinds Naran, and he began to feel his limbs twisting and ripping apart. Then he felt the hands of someone dragging him somewhere "stupid boy," he heard Kinich Ahau said before fainting.

Chapter 26

Against all odds, ancient gods have existed in the human world. Primarily because they became greedy. It wasn't enough to be powerful in their world; they wanted more. There were inconclusive things that Naran couldn't ignore. He couldn't die without having released those poor souls. With or without sins, it's not up to them to judge who deserves salvation and who doesn't. Hence the need to give them freedom at any cost. But how? His body didn't respond, and he wasn't sure if he was dead. It never occurred to him what would happen if he killed a god whose divinity was lacking, making him more human.

"Try opening your eyes" the voice sounded familiar and seemed distant. Naran's brain felt like a smudge of mod where such command, even if it was simple, felt impossible. He tried several times to do as instructed until he was able to see Kinich Ahau looking at him with concern. "Was dying your intention, foolish boy!" he sounded worried for Naran's wellbeing.

He is pretending. Thought Naran as he tried to step out of Kinich Ahau's hands. "What happened?" he said, looking around at what appears to be a chantli

"The only way to make sure your body didn't dissolve was to

drag you inside this tzacualli" Naran couldn't believe that Kinich Ahau trapped himself to save him. "What were you thinking?!" he said, and again he sounded like a father who is worried for his child.

However, this does not make amends for what he put him through "Why do you care?"

Kinich Ahau sighs, "you are my son, and despite what you might think, I never had intentions of hurting you."

Naran tried sitting up and lost his balance. Unfortunately for him, Kinich Ahau helped him, and since his strength hasn't come back yet, he let him. "Then what exactly did you want from me?" ask Naran once seated.

"Souls. Only you could gather them"

"Why?"

"Your half divinity made you the only half-human that could hold Quetzalcoatl." Saying the name of once, his former friend made his voice quaver. Quickly he clears his throat and continues, "and since you are human, it means you can touch the iztli."

Basically, I was born cursed. Thought Naran, feeling his entire life a lie. "All this to get more power!" clenching his hands, trying his best to avoid the tears coming out.

"Power is everything for my kind, and if I consume those souls, I could overthrow the strongest god."

"Then what?"

"Then-"

"Then you would go and eradicate another race or species, or whatever" tears fall "it's a never-ending story," said Naran with a trembling voice, clearing the tears. It didn't matter if Kinich Ahau saved him. Many people have perished because of him. Naran would never forgive him for that. However, he had to get information, and there is no point in being subtle anymore. "How can I free the souls?" there was no answer. "Tell me how!" Naran's strong voice made the entire tzacualli tremble

"I will never tell you," said Kinich Ahau, avoiding eye contact.

"Why not?"

"Naran, you won. I am trapped in this place!" motioning with his hands the entire area, "I cannot get out. Isn't this what you wanted?"

The god's resistance infuriated him to the point of launching punches at his face. He is trapped here, unable to do anything; his plan failed, yet he still wants to pull strings and decides what Naran can't and cannot do. Such stubbornness reminded Naran of himself. *I guess now I know from whom I got it.* The thought made him think of his mother, and his heart began to tremble. He couldn't hold it anymore. Tears flowed out "why did she have to die?" he said with a broken voice, holding the clothes of Kinich Ahau, "Why?" he fell to his knees. What happened next made Naran gasp.

Kinich Ahau holds him in a tight embrace like his mother used to do "I'm sorry it was the only way."

"What?" said Naran pushing him away

"I needed to awaken your divinity" he tried reaching Naran again. "If I didn't, you would have to remain a human."

"Get away from me!" Naran stood up quickly. "You made me kill my mother?!"

"You know very well that that is not what happened."

"She died to protect me. What difference does it make? I was the cause of her death!" his voice resounded all around.

"Please just listen to me!" said Kinich Ahau begging for the first time

"Why didn't you let me die?" he said, trying to hold his sobs to a minimum

"Naran, you are my son-"

"That didn't stop you before."

"But you didn't die, did you?!" The god turns around and calms himself before facing Naran again. "I might have had to push your mother to the point of giving her life up for yours," he took a deep breath, "but I needed to keep you safe."

"I kill innocent people because of you!"

"Yes, that's also my crime, and I don't regret it because it was the only way to make you this." He gestures to Naran's entire body. "To make sure you would become immortal and stay forever."

"With you?" said Naran, to which Kinich Ahau kept silent. Laughter erupted, shocking Kinich Ahau. Of all the reactions, he didn't imagine this one. "This is why you and Quetzalcoatl are made for each other," the laughter died down "both of you wanted more than you should," he said as he turned towards the farthest corner.

Kinich Ahau stood there helplessly, looking at the ground. "So, what" he turns to see the back of Naran. "Isn't this worth doing for someone you love and care"

"That's where you are wrong" Naran sat on the floor "that is not love," he said without breaking eye contact with Kinich Ahau.

"Teach me then," Naran chuckled at his comment and watched him sit down. "It seems we will be here for a long time, so why don't you teach me what love is."

"You are the one trap here. I could step out at any moment I want."

Kinich Ahau disapproved with his head. "Naran, she is gone. She gave you a chance to live, and you are going to throw it away?" As much as Naran hated to admit, Kinich Ahau is right. He can't die just like that. Nevertheless, this means they will live for centuries watching the earth evolve.

Hopefully, humans will come back at some point, except for the thousands of souls unaware that they are inside a relic made by a god from human objects. Surprisingly, the ruthless god who made all this cannot see his son die before his eyes. They were placed in the middle ground, forced to coexist.

Chapter 27

Naran meets his father without warning or heads up. On top of that, his father is considered an ancient god in the human world. No Teopixqui could have ever predicted that a god and a human would be trapped at some point in history. Although it would be more accurate to say that while this tzacualli represents the prison for a god, it's also the only thing keeping the human alive.

Naran never wondered about his father. He simply assumed someone had taken advantage of his poor mother, left her pregnant, and exiled her from the altepetl due to the social ranks. When he started to work in the crop fields, curiosity struck him. Being that close to the altepetl also meant he was closer to his father. He snuck into the higher ranks chantli trying to find a clue. Unfortunately, the expedition finished early, and he was caught. His mother always spoke highly of the Tecuhtli. Sadly, he did nothing to stop the Teopixqui. He stood there watching how his mother exchanged her life for his son. The wretched Teopixqui, unsatisfied with the outcome, forces Naran to finish his mother's life. With the tecpatl on his hand and his mother telling him everything would be fine; he knew he would rather die than continue. However, in a split second, his mother made a choice for him. And all because he was curious about someone who never cared for him.

His life has turned upside down since then. Whether his mother did this out of love forced him to live with the consequences of his actions. From that moment, he stopped believing in the sacrificial love that Quetzalcoatl and Kinich Ahau so proudly profess. If he had died as it was meant to be, none of this would have happened. Ironically his parents, without planning it, saved his life only to condemn him and everyone else.

This kept rumbling in Naran's head, making him question what else did Kinich Ahau do. "That day when the Teopixqui return early. Did you make that happen?" said Naran with a neutral voice.

"Yes," Kinich Ahau looks at him. "If that day didn't have to happen, you would have remained a human, and being human is a weakness."

Naran chuckled, "didn't you tell Quetzal to assume responsibility for his actions?"

"That's what I'm doing."

"You want me to believe you did that to assure I would live forever?"

"That's right."

"Well, it seems you didn't do a good job," said Naran with a smirk. Thinking of Kinich Ahau's response made it clear he was unbothered by the consequences that his actions cause. This infuriated Naran that he hit the floor with his palm. "You did that because it was the only way your plan could work!" he said.

Startling the god and forcing him to speak up. "Alright," he said with confidence, "I want to have everything. I wanted my son with me forever, and I wanted to gain power." There was no trace of sorrow or guilt in his voice.

"Seem wanting everything made you choose-"

"And I don't regret it," said Kinich Ahau quickly without hesitation.

"You hated Quetzal this much?" said Naran smiling and looking at him with disbelief

"Is not like-"

"Of all the humans, you choose her," said Naran interrupting Kinich Ahau just like he did. *How can he be this arrogant? For some reason, I thought he would be able to see all the hurt he had caused.* Thought Naran with frustration.

"I envy him," he sighs, defeated. "Blinded by that emotion, I made him watch all her deaths except for this one." He stood up. "I erase his memories with the Lihtnao each time." He looks down. "So that every time would feel to him like the first one." A small smile appears "that was all I did for decades until I notice he was regaining power." The smile disappears. "I couldn't figure out how he was doing it, so I had to stop because if I continued, he would have regained his original form. That's when the experiments began." He walked to the wall and rested against it. "I was giving up. Then I heard the prayers of your mother, and that's when all of this happened" he locked eyes with Naran. "I decided not to tell him. I knew if I had told him, you were my son, he would have killed you." He chuckled. "He ended up killing you but for other reasons. It took a lot of my energy to bring you back. Thankfully he didn't try again once I told him you were her." Crossing his arms on his chest, he waited for Naran's response.

"He didn't kill me," said Naran feeling his heart shatter a bit more

He looked at Naran with a calm expression. "I don't have any secret motives to lie to you. I told you. You won"

And why do I get the feeling that I actually lost? "Why are you telling me all this?" said Naran almost in a whisper

"Truth is the only thing I can give you."

Naran took this as an opportunity "then tell me how to free the souls?"

Kinich Ahau's lips turned into a thin line, and he clenched his hands "you need to summon the sword and destroy it," he said after some time.

Naran stood up quickly and summoned his sword just like Xoaltentli told him, yet nothing happened.

"It won't work here," said Kinich Ahau, "you need to be outside this tzacualli."

Immediately Naran walks to the door, but Kinich Ahau blocks him. "Let me go!" said Naran, fighting back.

"If you die, your mother and Quetzalcoatl's death would mean nothing. Is that what you want?"

Naran stops. *I can't keep thinking about the past. What is done is done.* By now, every human had died, every chantli burned down and every altepetl empty. *I need to at least try.* "Thousands of souls are more important than two," said Naran with confidence, knowing that his mother would have agreed with him.

"Alright, go ahead," said Kinich Ahau, stepping aside, "but this won't prevent others from coming and trying to do what I did." Naran stops. "What do you mean by that?"

"Out there, are probably a few shadows of what used to be gods roaming around."

"Didn't you kill them?" said Naran feeling anxious

"If I knew Xoaltentli and I do know him very well. I'm sure he brought a few back."

Naran's eyes widened. "How is that possible?"

"Didn't Quetzal tell you about the relics?"

Naran noded. "But he said Lihtnao was the only one that survives, and you have it."

"They were mortal relics created, just like the sword I gave you," Kinich Ahau rested against the wall knowing Naran would not leave. "They were forged by someone of my kind. I dispose of him. However, seeing Xoaltentli and the amount of power he had, he must have known where these relics are hiding."

"I kill him, so it's fine," said Naran turning to the exit.

"You kill one and only because he has possessed a human for far too long" he put a hand on Naran's shoulder. "Out there, shadows of pure energy are waiting for humans to appear again," he said, making Naran step back into the middle.

Thinking that there was no guarantee that the souls once free would be left alone or that things would be better when the humans start to appear. Naran wanted these gods out of his world to give humans a chance. Yet, it seems at this rate, history would repeat itself.

Up until now, things have been in his favor since he managed to consume a god, kill one and trap another one, who had a relic. Nevertheless, if what Kinich Ahau says is true, then it means that many gods are waiting for humans to show up to possess them. Not to mention that Kinich Ahau said 'relics' meaning more than one. "What do these relics do?" ask Naran, trying to stay calm for the response.

"It varies if it is a human or a god who is using it. It also depends on who is being used against. Tzatetl, for example, is a mortal relic that could maintain a low-rank god into an animal form, and since I have that one, no human got a chance to use it," said Kinich Ahau as he sat down. "If they were divine relics then that's a whole different story"

I'm guessing those are more powerful and harmful. "How many relics do you possess?"

"Three. Lihtnao, Tzatetl, and the sword I gave you."

This made Naran search for a clue or a way out. "Are you certain there are no divine relics left, just Lihtnao?"

"Yes," said Kinich Ahau watching Naran carefully

"How many mortal relics are there?"

"Ten or less. Most of them got destroyed," his face turning rigid, "but after seeing Xoaltentli, it's hard to say."

"What do you mean?" Naran tenses as he remembers how worried Kinich Ahau looked when he saw Xoaltentli.

"When he is weak, he does harmless things like getting in your dreams. When he is powerful, he can regenerate things from past thoughts or dreams. He could alter reality to make someone see what they fear or long for the most." He clenched his fist as if he

remembered something. "This illusion is also harmless unless he wants to lure you. If you realize it's fake, then nothing happens, but if you are caught, then it could trap you with no return."
The logging in his face meant he also was affected by Xoaltentli. This information made Naran recall the writing in the three and all the mythical things that happened when he was around Xoaltentli. *He tricked me. This whole time he used me to get closer to Kinich Ahau and the sword.* "It doesn't make sense. If what Xoaltentli wanted was the souls. Why did he wait until I was with you?"

"We had some unresolved business. He was more focused on revenge than on power. Idiot," said Kinich Ahau with a mischievous smile.

That idiot was powerful enough to break a sweat in Kinich Ahau. Thought Naran as he sat across the god. "How is it possible that he was that powerful and yet be human enough for me to kill him?"

"He was among the low rank, and that means that their abilities are weaker or sometimes affect them as well, like Quetzal. He also saw humans as creatures, just like you." *Seems that every time he mentions Quetzal, his voice cracks a little.* "His was mostly focused on the mind of his victim, turning his own mind into chaos and exposing himself."

That's how I was able to hurt him. "If he was low-rank, how was he so powerful now?" Naran knew it didn't matter anymore to know these things but it was the only distraction he could have. Kinich Ahau looks at his hands. "If you kill one of my kind you get to keep their essence. My intentions were to kill Xoaltentli so that I could refill the energy I used when I brought you back from death," he said, looking at Naran.

"I never ask you to save me," said Naran, defensible

"I know, and I'm not blaming you," he smiled. "I'm simply sharing what my plans were," the more they chatted, the less Naran felt threatened, and this made him feel ashamed. After all the death and destruction Kinich Ahau had made, he acted as if nothing had happened, making Naran feel secure and welcome in the process. *In the end, that is what he wanted to have me as his right arm and trust that whatever he did was to ensure I would be unharmed.* This is why Naran feels shame because he is starting to feel protected by the wrong person.

"I'm assuming that it wasn't the powerful god who got rid of the gods that broke the rules?" said Naran trying to focus on something else than his self-loathing

"That's correct."

"So how was Quetzal able to weaken you?"

"He did not weaken me!" said Kinich Ahau, making Naran move back a little. He then took a deep breath. "He absorbed part of my essences. Guess I always end up underestimating him"

Then everything made sense. "You did all this not out of envy but of fear. That Quetzal could regain himself and destroy you." Kinich Ahau remained silent, not denying what Naran said. This made him feel a momentary joy that then followed guilt. *How can I be content when all humankind has perished?* He remained quiet, repeating over and over all the death he has caused.

The sun rose and set so many times that Naran lost count.

Neither of them got hungry nor needed to sleep. It was torture not being able to die and not quite live.

Kinich Ahau kept looking at Naran now and then, making sure he was still breathing. They both seem to submerge in their thoughts.

Naran could feel his sins and guilt choking him down as he recalled the devastating things he had done. Worst of all, he came out unharmed and as the son of a god. This led him into such dense darkness that he couldn't distinguish between real and not. However, before his mind began to drift away, Naran made a decision. He knew that there were many more even though he got rid of three gods, a divine relic and two mortal relics. Gods will probably possess humans, and a few might find the rest of the relics. Yet, he had faith that someone would do what's needed to protect humankind once again.

Each day, he started to move towards the exit of the tzacualli, trying his best to not make any sound as he got closer. *I was never supposed to live. Death is the only way out.* "Having human frailty" said Naran pausing to look at his father "Gives me the right to decide when to cease existence and that would be your torture," he finishes with a small smile. Then with a quick move, he left knowing that Kinich Ahau couldn't save him.

Once more, he felt his insights burning. He summoned the word, focused everything he felt towards it, and before both the blade and Naran gave out, his last thought went to Quetzalcoatl.

Xoaltentli was right about the enlightenment that comes when death arrives. Naran was able to see his mother again with a new life, every child returning to their space in time. Every soul had an opportunity to live. Unfortunately, the relics would be found.